BEYOND THE HORIZONS

CAPT. SALINLAL. S

INDIA • SINGAPORE • MALAYSIA

*To the brave souls who crossed the
ocean's expanse*

*Guided by the stars, you charted
our dreams and destinies*

*Crafting the tales we share and
cherish*

Contents

Foreword

It is a privilege to write the foreword for *Beyond the Horizons*, a book that embodies the indomitable spirit of life at sea. Having spent decades navigating the world's oceans and paving the way as the first female merchant navy captain, I understand well the unique challenges and rewards that come with a maritime career.

This book resonates profoundly with me, not only because it reflects the dedication and resilience required in our profession, but also because it vividly illustrates the bonds formed between family, crew, and the sea. Captain Salinlal's narrative beautifully captures the essence of what it means to lead a life governed by tides, winds, and the weight of command. Through the experiences of Captain Bijoy and his crew, we are reminded of the precision, bravery, and teamwork essential to navigating both calm waters and turbulent seas.

Beyond the technical elements, this work is a tribute to the enduring human spirit—whether it is the excitement of new ventures, or the quiet resolve needed to confront the unexpected. It celebrates the joy of discovery and the deep, often unspoken, connections forged along the way.

For every seafarer, the horizon is not just a limit, but a symbol of what lies ahead—possibilities, challenges, and growth. This book captures that journey and serves as a timeless reminder that, though our ships may differ, the path we follow is shared.

With deep respect and admiration,
Capt. Radhika Menon
(India's First Female Merchant Navy Captain)

Foreward

Salinlal, a seasoned mariner and a budding author blends rich story telling with his experience of life at sea. He paints a vivid description of voyages infusing the story with his personal insights and experiences. His words bring to life the beauty and perils of maritime adventures while reflecting on family, responsibility, and leadership in a way only a mariner can.

Salinlal's creativity expression also finds an outlet in team sports, politics and Instagram. The discipline and dedication that allows him to persevere with his varied interests finds inspiration in Kalaripayattu, an art form that he keeps alive with dedication and regular practice.

Capt. Abhijith Balakrishnan

Acknowledgement

The sea has many faces: A nurturing mother to sailors, guiding them with a gentle embrace, or a furious force that draws sailors, sometimes down to its very depths.

A skilled sailor navigates through storms they cannot avoid and evades those they cannot endure. With every fall, their resolve strengthens. They see it as an opportunity for growth, which enables them to ride the crest, when it comes, with joy.

For me, sailing across the oceans was a dream. I believe that dreams are meant to be pursued, and this pursuit defines our existence; everything around us exists because someone dared to dream.

As you embark on this journey through my story, I invite you to step into the seafarer's shoes and immerse yourself in their experiences.

I extend my heartfelt gratitude to those who inspired and supported me along the way, and without whom my story would be incomplete. To my father, who now watches over me, encouraging me to write; to Vinayak, my editor, for shaping my work; and to every member of the Merchant Navy Officer's Cricket Club (MOCC), whose camaraderie transformed my life. Finally, to my family: your steadfast support has been my anchor.

As children, we gazed at the horizon, dreaming of the point where sky meets sea, and laid beneath the night sky, imagining a vast canopy enveloping us. Beyond those horizons lies not an end, but the beginning of a new adventure.

Capt. Salinlal.S

Prologue

Under the blazing blue sky, where the ancient walls of Galle Fort stand sentinel over untold secrets and stories, Captain Bijoy and his family stumbled upon a hidden gem—a luxurious resort, nestled deep within the verdant jungle, where time itself seemed to hold its breath. The air, though, was alive, thick with the intoxicating scent of Ceylon tea, mingling with the buttery warmth of freshly baked croissants, even as the earthy aroma of coffee wafted through the breeze. The melodies of exotic birds and the wild chatter of monkeys wove through the thick foliage, echoing in Bijoy's ears like a forgotten lullaby.

Despite Sri Lanka's tumultuous history, marked by internal conflicts, financial hardships, and war, its beauty remained timeless and irresistible. It was a land that could heal wounds, both seen and unseen.

"Dad, when will we go to your ship again?" Amiya's bright eyes, filled with the boundless curiosity of a six-year-old, sparkled as she asked the question, her small hands resting on the table in a cozy corner of the resort.

"You have to take us next time—and every time," she insisted, her voice carrying the urgency of a child's dreams.

It had been less than forty-eight hours since they disembarked from the ship in Colombo, yet Amiya's heart was already yearning for the sea once more. Bijoy, a seasoned seafarer with countless nautical miles behind him, smiled warmly at his daughter's eagerness. His wife, Priya, watched fondly as Amiya bounced with excitement.

Forty-five days earlier, Amiya and Priya had joined Bijoy on a voyage that began in California. From there, they navigated the engineering marvel of the Panama Canal and found themselves soaking in the vibrant energy of New York's Times Square. As they crossed the vast Atlantic Ocean, the echoes of the *Titanic* and Columbus whispered through their minds. Their journey led them to the grand stadium of Barcelona, resonating with the cheers of football fans, and then to the ancient splendour of Athens. They ventured further still, into the mystical lands of Egypt, where the timeless Pyramids stood as silent sentinels. After navigating the historic Suez Canal, they finally arrived in the vibrant city of Colombo.

"Amiya, your classes start next week. How will you go with Dad then?" Priya's voice broke through the reverie, gently reminding them of their routine on land.

"I want to go with Dad. You don't come," Amiya declared with a mischievous grin, climbing onto Bijoy's lap. "I want to see more places, have more ice cream, more chocolates," she continued, her imagination already whisking her away to new adventures.

Bijoy held a cigar between his fingers, though he did not intend to light it. His thoughts drifted back to 2014, the year he first donned the four golden stripes of a captain, commanding the good lady, the container ship *MV Kurasova*. The weight of responsibility and the thrill of commanding a ship had shaped his life ever since. He recalled the blend of pride and nervous excitement he felt as he assumed command for the first time.

Priya noticed the distant look in Bijoy's eyes, a look she had come to recognize. His mind was elsewhere, navigating the waters of memory. With Amiya's laughter echoing softly in the background, Priya reached out and gently touched Bijoy's hand. He continued to gaze at the endless blue sky.

Chapter 1

Where It All Started

—◆—

MV KURASOVA
DOCK: LONG BEACH
NAVIGATION BRIDGE
20TH OCTOBER 2014

In the soft light of dawn, the mammoth container ship *MV Kurasova* loomed large and majestic, her hull a sleek silhouette against the golden hue of the morning sky. She was a colossus of steel and engineering, her deck brimming with towering stacks of containers. Cranes swung into action with their long arms reaching out to unload and load cargo. Forklifts darted across the docks like busy ants, while the distant hum of engines blended with the cry of seagulls, creating a symphony of industry and nature.

"Ahoy, Second Officer, I trust all our voyage charts are shipshape," Captain Bijoy entered the navigation bridge, a cigar clasped between the fingers of one hand and a cup of Mexican coffee in the other. His eyes were heavy.

Second Officer Amol was diligently verifying the passage plan.

"Yes, Captain. The charts and publications are all up to date," he informed his superior, though he was a bit surprised to see him at this time after a night out party.

"Nice coffee mug," Amol continued after a pause, noticing the black cup in his hands, adorned with four golden stripes and the word 'CAPTAIN' inscribed on it.

"Thanks, mate. I found this fancy stuff in the pub last night," Bijoy responded, a hint of a smile tugging at his lips. "Any navigational warnings?" he asked, his tone shifting to a more serious note.

"We received an alert early this morning about military exercises along our route, necessitating a slight deviation from yesterday's route plan," Amol responded, indicating the position marked on the chart.

"Blast it! Another military exercise? They always send out these alerts, though I've yet to see one come in real ever since I was baptized in shipping sixteen years ago," Bijoy chuckled wryly. "How's the cargo operation faring? Will they finish on schedule?"

"I've heard the Third Officer's report; there are 460 containers remaining with only three cranes operational. The cargo agent assures us that the cargo operations will conclude by 1900 hours today," Amol relayed.

Captain Bijoy set his coffee mug down in the pantry and turned to face Amol. "However, we'll need to wait for low tide, so our departure can't be before 0300 hours."

"Low tide? To pass under Gerald Bridge?" Amol queried.

"Indeed. I've instructed the Chief Officer to maintain at least a two-meter clearance," Captain Bijoy responded, pouring himself another cup of coffee.

"He took on a bit more ballast water last night to ensure a two-and-a-half-meter clearance," Amol added.

"Ah, Gregory… a typical Ukrainian. He's never satisfied," Bijoy chuckled, and Amol joined in.

They peered through the bridge's expansive windows at the cargo operation below. Towering cranes stretched skyward like mechanical giants, their arms deftly plucking containers from the bustling port terminal below. Each steel container swung through the air before settling on the ship's deck. The third officer stood nearby, ensuring proper loading, while the chief electrician checked and connected the reefer containers. Teams of stevedores, clad in fluorescent vests and hard hats, moved around briskly. They secured each container with care, fastening heavy-duty straps and twist locks to ensure their cargo would weather the rigors of the Pacific Ocean. Millions of dollars' worth of goods were being loaded onto her, and they were expected to load a golden mark of full capacity: 14,000 containers. Chief Officer Gregory issued instructions over the VHF. He doesn't want to miss out on anything.

"Alright, Second, let's do the passage plan meeting after lunch," Captain Bijoy instructed, then departed the bridge holding the coffee mug in his hands.

The *MV Kurasova* was preparing for its voyage from Long Beach to Auckland, its cargo operations having spanned the last four days. While Long Beach offered the allure of Hollywood to most, seasoned mariners sought respite at Long Beach's most famous hangout, Firkin Pub, for a few quiet beers. Each shore leave marked a period of rejuvenation for sailors, a chance to reconnect with land after endless days on floating metal.

For Bijoy, this voyage marked the final stint of his first command. His contract had been tranquil thus far, each moment as captain a cherished experience. For every cadet joining the Merchant Navy, donning those decorated four golden stripes and the feathered cap was a dream come true. It was the captain's duty to safeguard his crew as long as there was water beneath the keel, even if the world stood still, and so far, he had fulfilled his duties admirably.

He was counting down the days until sign-off at the next port. Homecoming after his first command would be a proud moment for the family. Adding to the excitement, his wife, Priya, was six months pregnant, awaiting the arrival of their first child. A new life, conceived just before he joined the ship, was now waiting for his return.

Chapter 2

A Long-Cherished Dream

MEXICO
YELAPA BEACH
20TH OCTOBER 2014

At the tender age of sixty-seven, Edward Christabel and Thomas Williams, affectionately known as Christy and Willy, sat in quiet contemplation by the Pacific Ocean, their hands clasping Amstel beer cans and their eyes shielded by Ray-Ban aviators. Their bond, forged since their infancy, had weathered the passage of time without a single day's absence between them.

Their current reverie marked the culmination of a lifelong dream, a madcap journey spanning forty-five exhilarating days across Latin America. From daring treks through the vibrant Rainbow Hills to striking iconic poses beneath Rio's Christ the Redeemer, and later, sharing the passion of Boca Juniors fans at Pelusa's (Maradona) stadium. A motorbike ride in homage to Che Guevara's legendary travels had ignited memories of their youth, rekindled in their sixties.

Christabel, a prosperous real estate lawyer, and Williams, a retired distinguished professor of physics at Auckland University, and now his business partner, had set aside their busy work schedule for this six-week escapade. Now, perched on the precipice of another daring venture, they awaited the fulfillment of a long-cherished dream: crossing the vast Pacific Ocean.

Their ambition had materialized in the form of a majestic seventeen-meter yacht, the *Odyssey*, adorned with a pristine white hull and blue stripes. In light of their lack of navigational expertise beyond tranquil lakeside sails, they had secured the services of Juan Romis, a seasoned forty-five-year-old Mexican sailor. Finding a skipper willing to brave the Pacific's expanse aboard their modest vessel had been no small feat. But after three days of vigorous search and bargain in that beach city of Mexico, they had found Juan, who finally agreed when they promised him that he would get ownership of the *Odyssey* when they reached Auckland.

As they gazed steadfastly toward the horizon, contemplating the uncertainties of their impending voyage, Christy and Willy knew that life could transform drastically within the next three weeks. The risks were palpable, the stakes high, yet the prospect of becoming the first New Zealanders over sixty to conquer the Pacific fueled their determination.

In the peaceful hush of that ocean-view moment, with the sun casting its golden hues upon the water's surface, their glances spoke volumes. For Christy and Willy, this was not merely a voyage—it was a testament to the unwavering pursuit of dreams, no matter how improbable, and the enduring power of their friendship that had withstood the test of time.

It was their last night on land, and they decided to go out with a bang. The smoky aroma of barbeque filled the air, mingling with the sound of laughter and clinking beer bottles. They sat around a bonfire on the beach, its flames dancing against the darkening sky.

Music played from portable speakers, and they danced with wild abandon, their feet sinking into the cool sand. As the night wore on, their energy did not wane. If anything, it grew more vibrant. Stories and jokes of their forty-five-day trip were flying in the air. Finally, as the stars sparkled above and the bonfire burned low, Juan took charge. Gently, but firmly, he guided Christy and Willy to their rooms, one by one. In the quiet aftermath, the beach lay still, remnants of the celebration scattered around. The waves lapped gently at the shore, and the fire's embers glowed softly. The party had ended. The next party would be in Auckland, with the family, in three weeks, after conquering the mighty Pacific Ocean.

Chapter 3

Passage Planning

———◦◆◦———

MV KURASOVA
NAVIGATION BRIDGE
20ᵀᴴ OCTOBER 2014

The team assembled for the passage plan meeting after a light lunch, a critical ritual before any sea voyage. Captain Bijoy insisted on the presence of the chief engineer and the duty seamen, alongside the usual navigating officers. As always, Second Officer Amol was at the helm of preparations. He spread the navigation charts across the table.

The route from Long Beach to Auckland spanned fifty meticulously detailed charts, each one precisely marked with the necessary reports for various authorities and the areas to avoid due to navigational constraints. Within the company, it was common knowledge: if Amol prepared the passage plan, it would be flawless. He took immense pride in this reputation. His charts were so immaculate that even the most critical eyes were unable to find any faults.

Apart from his reputation as a perfectionist, Amol was also known for his quirks, particularly his obsession with sunglasses. Every three months, he refreshed his collection, and you'd never catch him without a pair—whether perched on his nose or resting on his head, no matter the time of day.

Captain Bijoy stood beside the chart table, a steaming mug of coffee in hand. "Gentlemen, we have about a fourteen-day voyage ahead of us. The weather is expected to be choppy for the first two days and calm after that," he announced.

"Chief, check the container lashings thoroughly. I don't want any of them falling into the sea on the way," Bijoy continued, his tone firm. "Then, as usual, move the mooring ropes to the store room after departure and ask the bosun to secure all loose items from the deck. Let us prepare for heavy weather."

Chief Officer Gregory nodded, although his mind was preoccupied with the cargo operation. Several reefer containers were being loaded, requiring extra care, lest there be a thousand questions to answer later.

"Second Officer, have you marked the positions to reduce speed for blue whale protection?"

"Yes, Captain," Amol replied, rattling off the numbers with practiced ease. "Twenty-five nautical miles off the Long Beach coast and forty nautical miles while approaching Auckland. We have to maintain a speed under ten knots."

"Very good. This is the season for blue whale migration, so we may see one or two along the coast. Keep an extra lookout for them. I don't want an issue with a whale on my bulbous bow," Captain Bijoy said, smiling.

"Captain, the whales will be underwater. Why do we have to detect them, and how?" Third Officer Andrei Kovalenko wanted to know. He had joined just the previous day, an overenthusiastic Bulgarian, or so it seemed at first impression.

"Third, whales are magnificent but peculiar creatures. This is their migration season, possibly to adjust to climate changes. Unfortunately, they do not realize that a mammoth ship might be cruising in their path, so they might inadvertently collide with us. While it is nearly impossible for us to detect them either visually or by radar, at least we can reduce the impact on them by moving slowly. That's why the authorities insist on speed reduction," Bijoy explained.

Andrei looked lost in thought.

Bijoy shifted the conversation, "How was your flight to Los Angeles? A long one, wasn't it? Did you get proper rest?"

"Yes, Captain. I had two days at a hotel, where I enjoyed a few beers and a good steak," Andrei replied, joyfully playing with a hand spinner.

"Hope you received a proper handover from the last Third Officer," Bijoy checked.

"Yes, but it seems he was just passing the time. No proper records and all equipment under his care is in bad shape," Andrei replied.

This remark raised a few eyebrows, and several sets of eyes turned towards Andrei. Everyone knew that the previous third officer had been a hard worker.

"Third Officer, there should not be any blame culture on my ship. I don't entertain it at all. Once you take over and sign the duties, no one else will come to rescue you from the responsibilities of your rank," Bijoy said sharply.

"Have you completed the familiarization process for new joiners?" he asked, after a pause.

"I will do it after departure," Andrei said in a low voice.

"No, it should be done right after this meeting. Don't you know the regulation? New crew members should familiarize themselves with emergency procedures within twenty-four hours of joining."

"I know, Captain."

"Then why was it not done?"

Though soft-spoken, Bijoy had to ensure clarity in certain matters, especially the bond between crew members and the on-board culture. Therefore, party spoilers had to be handled properly from the very outset.

The navigation bridge was completely silent.

After two sips of coffee, Bijoy turned to the chief officer. "We have taken some extra ballast water, haven't we?"

"Yes, Captain. 400 metric tonnes more than initially planned for. We can pump it out after reaching open sea. We will pass the two-and-a-half-meter clearance under Gerald Bridge."

"Very good, Chief. Keep everything recorded," Bijoy said, nodding.

Then, he moved to the chief engineer. "Were you out last night?"

Rajesh and Bijoy had been batchmates at the nautical institute and had climbed the ranks together. Though they were buddies ashore, on-board, they addressed each other formally, by rank.

"Yes, Captain, just for a couple of beers. Thanks to our excellent engine team, we completed the main engine maintenance by yesterday afternoon. Three days of hectic work. We were exhausted, so we decided to visit the pub in the evening."

"Oh, that's wonderful! Let's test the engine at maximum speed during this voyage. I'll try to secure extra working allowance for our crew," Captain Bijoy was pleased. The ship's engine had caused trouble on the previous voyage, prompting a request for shore assistance. But the chief engineer, Rajesh Kumar, had stepped in, promising to fix the issue if given enough time. Bijoy trusted 'superman' Rajesh, granted the time, and they had completed the job.

"By the way, did any good cricket players join the ship yesterday?" Bijoy teased.

Rajesh was a well-known cricket enthusiast. Whenever there was a crew change, his primary concern was finding new recruits who could join the Sunday cricket matches on-board. His expertise in main engine jobs took a back seat to his passion for the game.

The mood lightened as they discussed the passage plan in detail, covering weather and expected traffic. After forty-five minutes, Amol placed the charts back in the drawer.

"Alright, gentlemen, do we have enough stock of beer for three parties? The Chief Engineer and I will go home at the next port, so let us party hard."

'Aye aye, Captain!' the crew responded in unison.

Chapter 4

Off to Conquer the Pacific Ocean

YELAPA BOAT CLUB
MEXICO

The morning sun cast a golden glow over the marina as the *Odyssey* prepared for its ambitious journey across the Pacific Ocean. The air was thick with a mix of excitement and bittersweet emotion. On the dock, Juan Romis' family and a few close friends gathered, their faces a blend of pride, worry, and heartfelt goodbyes. Christy and Willy were making last-minute calls to their families from the public telephone booth. The three sailors had unanimously decided that there would be no alcohol until they reached Auckland.

Christy and Willy stepped aboard the *Odyssey*. It had only one bedroom with two bunks, and their belongings were minimal—just a few sets of warm clothes, gloves, and some satellite telephone calling cards. She was equipped with state-of-the-art technology. The luxurious saloon featured a large flatscreen TV and a selection of Hollywood movie DVDs, a small dining table with three chairs neatly arranged to one side. The galley was stocked with enough frozen food to last a month, ensuring easy meals during their time away from land. The bathroom was a tiny but functional space, eliciting a wink from Willy at Christy as he joked about how his six-foot-four-inch frame would fit.

The navigation station was a masterclass in nautical precision and design. It was a compact yet comprehensive hub of activity, where Juan could plot courses and track the yacht's progress across the vast ocean. A large chart table dominated the center of the station, its polished surface reflecting the soft glow of the overhead lights. Rolled-up nautical charts were neatly stacked in a holder to one side, each one detailing the safest passages through treacherous waters and marking the hazardous shoals and reefs that lay in wait.

Mounted above the chart table was an array of cutting-edge electronic equipment, a blend of tradition and technology. The GPS and chart plotter screens glowed with digital maps, constantly updating with the yacht's position, speed, and heading. Their current location was marked as a red dot in the marina of Mexico, poised to embark on a journey across the vast Pacific Ocean. The GPS and chart plotter would update their position every thirty seconds once they were out at sea. Nearby, the radar screen swept in silent vigilance, revealing the unseen obstacles and other vessels hidden by darkness or fog. The VHF radio, a lifeline to the outside world, crackled intermittently with the voices of distant mariners and coastguards, offering a reassuring connection to humanity amid the isolation of the ocean. Alongside it, the Automatic Identification System (AIS) displayed the movements of nearby ships, each blip on the screen representing a potential ally or a hazard.

The skipper's chair, a comfortable swivel seat upholstered in weather-resistant fabric, was positioned perfectly to allow a commanding view of all the instruments while providing a direct sightline to the chart table. From this vantage point, Juan could oversee every aspect of the yacht's journey, making real-time adjustments to the course and ensuring the safety of all on-board. He placed a small, framed photo of his family near the steering wheel, a constant reminder of his wife, Maria, and daughter, Adriana, smiling back at him.

The *Odyssey* bobbed gently in the water, its sleek lines and polished hull gleaming in the sunlight. Flags fluttered in the gentle breeze, adding a festive touch to the moment. On the dock, Maria held their young child, her face a mixture of pride and concern.

"Be safe, love," she whispered, her voice trembling as she handed him a small good-luck charm. The skipper, strong and reassuring, kissed her gently and then bent down to hug his daughter. "Take care of Mommy for me, okay?" he said with a warm smile, ruffling the child's hair.

As the *Odyssey*'s engine roared to life, the sound was both a promise of adventure and a reminder of the distance soon to separate them. Juan gave a final wave, his heart heavy with the farewells but buoyed by the excitement of the voyage. "I'll be back before you know it," he shouted, trying to keep his tone light. The yacht began to move, slowly at first, then picking up speed as it left the dock. For the three men on-board, the journey was just beginning, filled with the promise of open seas and new horizons.

When the *Odyssey* disappeared over the horizon, Maria turned to Adriana, drawing strength from their shared bond. The journey across the Pacific was a test of endurance and courage, not just for those on the yacht, but also for those who stayed behind, keeping the home fires burning and their hearts hopeful.

Chapter 5

Underway!

—◦❖◦—

MV KURASOVA
DEPARTURE

Chief Officer Gregory walked briskly along the wharf, the crisp night air invigorating his senses. The cargo operation had finally concluded at midnight, and the crew now awaited the pilot. Confirming everything in order on the shipside, Gregory looked over the immense *MV Kurasova*—a veritable floating island at 366 meters long and 48 meters wide, the fully-loaded vessel loomed majestically against the night sky and the projected lights from the cranes.

Gregory reported the ship's draft to the captain, who stood on the bridge dressed in his crisp black trousers and white shirt, adorned with the captain's stripes. From his vantage point, thirty-five meters above the water level, the captain surveyed the stacks of containers one last time.

With port clearance in hand, the mooring stations and engine room fully manned, the crew settled into a waiting game. They were waiting for the pilot's arrival, whose job was to help the captain guide the ship out of the port and congested waters.

The pilot reached the wharf after about twenty-five minutes, a small, elderly man wearing a beret. He eyed the steep aluminum ladder attached to the ship's side and, with a nonchalant air, lit a cigar, puffing away as he made his way toward the gangway. Climbing it with the measured pace of a man well versed in the rhythms of the sea, he was met at the top by the bosun and the third officer. They greeted him with polite nods and brief, efficient words before the third officer guided him down the alleyway and into the elevator.

Meanwhile, the bosun and another seaman remained at the gangway, awaiting the captain's orders. Moments later, the command came through the radio: "Secure the gangway", as the last person, the pilot, boarded the ship.

With great care, the bosun engaged the winch. The gangway rose steadily, creaking and groaning before locking firmly into place. Then, he headed towards the mooring station.

Inside the elevator, the third officer and the pilot ascended in silence, the hum of the machinery a comforting constant. As the doors slid open, the pilot stepped out onto the navigation bridge, greeted by the sight of Captain Bijoy.

"Good morning, Captain. Apologies for the delay. The channel was busy with another vessel berthing behind your good lady," the pilot greeted Bijoy.

"That's quite alright, Mr. Pilot. I was watching that vessel's movements. Would you care for a strong cup of coffee?" Captain Bijoy offered.

"Indeed, Captain. Black, no sugar, no milk," the pilot responded.

Bijoy turned to his third officer. "Andrie, prepare a good cup of coffee for the pilot."

While the third officer prepared the coffee, the captain and the pilot discussed the plan to guide the big lady *MV Kurasova* into the open sea.

"You'll have two tugs to assist with unberthing. The traffic is free in the channel. No vessels inbound. Yes, there may be a few leisure crafts, but chances are low now at this hour of the night. Your sailing draft of fourteen meters gives us a clear margin under Gerald Bridge," the pilot explained.

"Understood, Mr. Pilot. All checks have been completed as per United States laws, including engine tests ahead and astern. Everything is in good order. The crew is standing by for your instructions," Captain Bijoy confirmed.

Coffee in hand, they moved to the bridge wing to have a better sight of the ship's side. The tugs, secured alongside the vessel, stood ready.

"Gentlemen, forward and aft, standby for stations," Captain Bijoy commanded.

The chief officer managed the forward station while the second officer took charge at the aft. The vessel was secured with fourteen mooring ropes, each thicker than a man's thigh, seven at each end. Handling those ropes under tension is not easy. A small error in this critical operation could spell disaster.

"Let go all ropes forward and aft," Captain Bijoy instructed, after getting confirmation from the pilot.

The chief officer and the second officer acknowledged over the radio, releasing the ropes from the winches.

As the ropes slackened, the mooring men—burly, efficient figures—released the eye of the ropes from the bollards.

"All ropes released forward," the chief officer reported, echoed by the second officer from aft.

"Thank you. Vessel underway. Report back once all ropes are on-board," Captain Bijoy responded. Now the vessel was free and floating, detached from the shore.

Minutes later, the officers reported that all ropes had been taken back on-board using winches. The tugs began pulling the ship from the berth.

"Dead slow ahead," Captain Bijoy commanded.

The third officer repeated the order and moved the telegraph forward, igniting the engine and propeller. The *MV Kurasova* began to move, water splashing from the propeller, creating a strong wake. The third officer watched the charts carefully, ensuring the movement of the vessel along the planned route, and plotting its position frequently.

After a while, the imposing silhouette of the Gerald Bridge loomed ahead, its steel structure standing stark against the early morning sky. The pilot, calm and composed, expertly aligned the ship's position to pass beneath the bridge's center, where a blue light flashed rhythmically. The steering seaman, his hands steady on the wheel, executed the manoeuvre with the precision of threading a needle.

On the deck, the chief officer stood at the edge, his eyes fixed on the bridge's underside. He had run the calculations a hundred times, ensuring the clearance on paper, but now it was time to witness it in reality. The seconds stretched into what felt like decades, each one filled with the tension of anticipation.

As the massive *MV Kurasova* inched closer, the entire crew held their breath, the bridge's girders seeming perilously close. The chief officer's heart pounded in his chest, his mind racing through every possible outcome. The captain, the pilot, and the crew watched with bated breath; every eye trained on the narrowing gap.

Finally, the vessel cleared the bridge. A collective sigh of relief swept through the vessel. Captain Bijoy commented over the radio, "Bravo, Chief Officer. Good job."

After an hour of navigating through the coastal waters with experienced ease, the *MV Kurasova* finally reached the open sea. The pilot, having fulfilled his duty, prepared to disembark.

"All the best, Captain, for the voyage. Please adjust speed for my disembarkation," the pilot said, his tone professional yet warm.

"Thank you, Mr Pilot. I'll adjust the speed." Bijoy turned to Andrei. "Escort the pilot, please."

Andrei nodded and led the pilot down the gangway. A bright orange pilot boat approached, slicing through the waves. As the pilot boat drew alongside the massive vessel, the pilot descended the ladder with the agility of a man accustomed to the sea's capricious nature. The crew of the pilot boat, synchronized and precise, secured him quickly. With a final wave, the pilot boat pulled away, bobbing briskly over the waves, and made its way back to the pilot station.

After ensuring everything was clear, Captain Bijoy gave the long-awaited command.

"Full speed ahead."

The third officer relayed the command, and the ship's engines roared to life, their hum growing into a powerful, steady thrum. The *MV Kurasova* surged forward, cutting through the waves with a grace that belied its immense size.

As the vessel accelerated, Long Beach and other familiar coastal landmarks gradually receded, becoming mere specks on the horizon. The vast, open ocean stretched out before them, an endless expanse of deep blue, inviting and daunting in equal measure. Captain Bijoy remained on the bridge, the wind tousling his hair, his eyes scanning the horizon. The voyage across the mighty Pacific was a monumental task. The ship, a floating colossus, responded to his command with obedient power, its path now clear and unencumbered.

The sun began to rise, casting a golden glow over the water, heralding the start of a new day and an exciting new chapter in their journey.

Chapter 6

Navigating Under the Stars

⸻ ◆ ⸻

There is a timeless allure to chasing dreams, especially when the odds seem stacked against you. Legends, as they say, are those who dare to defy the norms, who set out to accomplish what others might deem impossible. The trio aboard that modest yacht—Christy, Willy, and Juan—embodied this spirit. Their bucket list was not just a list of fleeting desires; it was a lifelong ambition that had matured with them, each passing year only strengthening their resolve.

For four days, they had been making steady progress across the vast Pacific. The gorgeous *Odyssey*, belying her size, sliced through the open waters with purpose. The occasional aches in their aging bodies were mere reminders of the years they had lived, but these were minor inconveniences in the grand scheme of things. That morning, the engine had sputtered, showing signs of trouble. Juan had managed to get it running again, though he knew it was only a temporary fix. *"I'll need to do a full overhaul once we reach the next port,"* he said to himself, mentally noting the repairs needed. "An engine with a few hiccups is better than one with no issues at all," he had told the Auckland duo. Despite the physical toll, their minds remained sharp and focused, driven by the unwavering dream of crossing the Pacific.

Their journey was marked by the occasional sight of a massive cargo ship on the horizon, its smokestack leaving a faint trace in the sky, and by the joyous leaps of dolphins at their bow. However, beyond these, it was just the three of them and the endless expanse of the ocean. Every night, they would reach out to their loved ones via satellite phone, a small comfort and a reminder of the world they had stepped away from. Their mission was clear: to live the adventure they had always dreamed of, together, with nothing but the open sea ahead of them.

Christy was often lost in thought, his eyes scanning the night sky, captivated by the stars and their ancient myths. Willy, ever the pragmatist, found amusement in Christy's musings, often teasing him about being a fox looking at the moon.

"Willy," Christy began on that clear night, "we're in the southern part of the Earth now as proper navigators. Navigation is an art, and navigators are the true artists—the most ancient art form known to man. Imagine a time when these gems in the sky were the only guides. How many brave souls must have navigated uncharted waters with nothing but the stars to light their way?"

"Christy, give it a rest. I don't want to fall asleep to your lectures tonight," Willy protested, though a smile played on his lips.

Juan, the real artist among them, could not resist joining in the conversation. Navigation had been his life's work, his passion.

"The pole star is crucial for those sailing in the Northern Hemisphere. If you stand in the position of the crucifixion facing the pole star, your right arm points east, your left west, and your feet south," he explained, his voice steady and authoritative.

"But how do we find the pole star?" William inquired, genuinely curious now.

"Look up at the sky for a constellation shaped like a question mark," Juan said. "Draw an imaginary line from the head of the question mark, and it will lead you to the pole star. Unfortunately, in the Southern Hemisphere, we can't see it."

"Oh, the *saptarshis* of Indian mythology!" William exclaimed, a glimmer of recognition in his eyes.

"I don't know about that," Juan replied with a chuckle. "We call it Ursa Major, the Great Bear constellation. According to legend, the bear is trying to reach a beehive in the sky to get honey. The stars of Ursa Major and the pole star represent the bear and the beehive. The bear has been trying to get the honey there in the sky for millions of years but has never succeeded."

"Interesting," Christy said thoughtfully.

"There are many constellations we can see in the sky here," Juan, the quiet Spaniard, pointed to the Scorpion constellation, his thick accent adding a musical quality to his words. He shared the legends associated with it, stories passed down through generations.

"Stars are the searchlights lit by our ancestors," Christy said, his voice reverent. "They guide us to the future."

That night, they shared tales under the canopy of the night sky, the loneliness of the vast ocean momentarily forgotten. The immense depth of 3,000 meters beneath their boat seemed less daunting as they found solace in the ancient stories of the stars. Their journey across the Pacific continued, not just a physical voyage, but a journey through time, connecting them to the explorers of old and the infinite mysteries of the universe.

Chapter 7

Drifting Through the Steel

MV KURASOVA
PACIFIC OCEAN

Five days had slipped by since the celebrations at Long Beach. Sailors, resilient and adaptive, swiftly settled into their routines, attending to the 'good lady', as they affectionately called the ship. Regardless of the circumstances, the ship must sail and perform her duties.

The first two days after departure were a grueling trial for the crew. A low-pressure weather system had settled ominously over the western American coast, whipping the sea into a fury and unleashing ferocious winds. Captain Bijoy, ever vigilant, was forced to navigate, constantly adjusting the ship's heading and speed to keep her on course. One wave after another crashed violently against the bow, sending plumes of icy spray cascading across the deck, as if nature itself was testing their resolve. The power of the winds was immense, shaking the very core of the vessel.

Containers stacked high on deck groaned under the strain, the heavy clank of the lashing turnbuckles echoing through the chaos. Yet, as sailors must, they endured, bound by duty to face the tempest head-on. Through grit and determination, they sailed through it, emerging victorious on the other side, the ship steady once more, and the crew hardened by the trial.

At precisely 0630 hours, the ship's daily ritual began. Captain Bijoy, a man of few words and many responsibilities, made his way to the Navigation Bridge, a sanctum of steel and glass perched high above the deck. The chief officer, Gregory, already on navigation duty, greeted him with a nod, his robust Ukrainian accent mingling with the familiar scent of strong black coffee. Shortly thereafter, the chief engineer, Rajesh Kumar, would join them, fresh from his morning workout in the gym. As the three exchanged light-hearted banter, the cadet, still green around the edges but eager to prove himself, busied himself with cleaning the bridge. Bosun Lewis, a man who had seen more years at sea than most men on that ship had seen birthdays, entered the bridge at 0645 hours, his eyes immediately catching the small section of the floor that the cadet had missed, Without a word, he made a subtle but decisive gesture, a silent signal with his hand and eyes that only the cadet noticed.

"Good morning, Bosun," Gregory greeted him.

"Good morning, Chief. Good morning, everybody," he replied cheerfully.

As the bosun, Lewis was the linchpin in the maintenance of the *MV Kurasova*, the man who ensured that every bolt was tightened, every surface cleaned, and every piece of machinery well-oiled and ready to face the rigors of the sea. His efforts had not gone unnoticed; the praise from the United States Coast Guard during their last port inspection in Long Beach was a testament to his dedication.

Gregory and Lewis discussed the maintenance plan for the day—a list that included checking the container lashings, de-rusting the main deck, and lubricating the deck machinery. These were routine tasks, but vital ones, for the ship's well-being was their responsibility.

"Bosun, let's plan to shift the oil drums to the engine room today if the weather is good," Rajesh suggested, his voice tinged with the practical concerns of a man whose life revolved around machinery and maintenance.

"Let's schedule that for tomorrow, Chief. We will need extra time today to check and tighten the container lashings. Some of them may have come loose with the bad weather," Gregory said, already calculating the hours needed to finish the day's tasks.

"No problem, let's do it tomorrow then."

"Bosun, we need some paint for the engine room. I will send the crew to you at tea time," Rajesh continued.

"Okay, Sir. I will arrange it," Lewis replied, his tone matter-of-fact. The paint locker was his domain, and he took pride in maintaining it with the same meticulous care he applied to everything else on the ship.

The handheld radio crackled to life, breaking the stillness of the morning with the voice of the Electrical Officer.

"Bridge, this is the Electrical Officer calling."

"Yes, Electrical Officer, go ahead," Gregory responded, grabbing the radio from its cradle.

"All reefer containers are checked and temperature monitored. All in good order," the electrical officer reported, his voice carrying the weight of responsibility that came with such a crucial task. A small but significant reassurance given to the high-value cargo of medicines they were transporting in refrigerated containers to New Zealand.

"Thank you," Gregory replied, his mind moving on to the next item on the endless list of duties that defined life aboard the *MV Kurasova*.

Bijoy, who had been silently observing the exchange, made a mental note of the day's maintenance plan. It was essential to keep the ship in good condition—her well-being was paramount.

After the discussion with the chief officer, Lewis turned to the captain, his voice carrying the tone of a man with something important to say.

"Sir, I have a request to make," he began, his words carefully chosen.

"Tell me, Bosun," Captain Bijoy responded.

"The seaman Ivan is asking for an early sign-off in the next port," Lewis continued.

"Why? He has not completed his contract," Bijoy said, raising an eyebrow in surprise.

"He has some medical emergency at home," Lewis informed him, his tone respectful but firm.

"Medical emergency? Oh God, what happened? Is there any major concern?" Bijoy asked.

"Sir, his wife is pregnant," Lewis replied in a low voice.

"Pregnant? Bosun, being pregnant is not a medical emergency; it is the result of planned hard work," Bijoy laughed, the sound a rare break from his usual stoic demeanor, and everyone joined in.

"Let me check with the office what can be done," he assured, his voice softening as he considered the request. The crew was his responsibility, and he knew the weight of their concerns.

Lewis left the bridge, his mind returning to the tasks at hand.

"Hey, Chief, have you received the salary in your account?" Bijoy asked Gregory, casual, but tinged with concern.

Gregory, a man whose life was divided between the vastness of the ocean and the turmoil of his homeland, was not one to complain easily. Yet the weight of his worries was evident in the tightness of his brow and the fatigue in his eyes. The ongoing conflict in his country was more than just a distant news story.

"The account works well, but the situation in my country continues the same. My wife has to stand in queue even to withdraw a hundred dollars from the bank," Chief Officer Gregory replied, his thick accent unable to mask the frustration and worry that had become his constant companions.

The silence lingered for a few seconds before he continued, frustration evident in his tone. "I've got money in the account and I'm working hard for it, but I can't use it the way I want."

"Oh, that is bad. Why don't you plan to shift to some other country?" asked Rajesh, his voice filled with the pragmatic concern of a man who had seen his share of hardships.

"No, I hope things will be better soon," Gregory replied, his tone resolute but laced with uncertainty.

By 0745 hours, the third officer, Andrei, arrived on the bridge, his youthful energy a contrast to the seasoned calm of the men already there. He took over the duty, the navigational watch, his eyes scanning the radar screen, which was mercifully clear of any approaching vessels. It was a small measure of comfort and allowed the others to leave the bridge for breakfast.

They took the stairs instead of the elevator, arriving at the mess room—a grand and meticulously designed space. The room was adorned with rich wooden paneling and elegant carpeting. On one side stood a round table with four high-backed leather chairs, while the other side featured a long table surrounded by eight finely crafted chairs. Each place setting was carefully arranged, with gleaming silverware and crystal glasses. The tablecloths were of soft linen, adding a touch of luxury. The spoons and forks neatly arranged on the table glowed under the soft pendant lights and wall sconces. On one wall, a large portrait of the ship, captured at her launch ten years ago in a Korean shipyard, hung proudly, its golden frame reflecting the room's light.

The three of them sat at the round table. The atmosphere was relaxed yet purposeful after two days of bad weather.

The steward served their breakfast without disturbing the conversation. Captain Bijoy, always mindful of the ship's needs, instructed the steward to summon the Chief Cook.

"Call the Chief Cook, please," he said.

"Ok, Sir," the steward replied before leaving the mess room.

A few minutes later, the heavy-built figure of the chief cook, Nikolay Plaman, filled the doorway. A Bulgarian by birth, Nikolay was a man whose physical presence was as commanding as the tattoos that adorned his six-foot-six-inch frame. At fifty-five, he was a man of contrasts—his rock star appearance belied by the warmth and generosity that made him a beloved figure on-board.

"Yes, Captain, did you call me?" Nikolay asked, his voice deep and resonant.

"Yes, Nikolay, we are planning to lift provisions from the next port. Give me the inventory and the request list by tomorrow," Captain Bijoy instructed him.

"Okay, I will prepare and give it to you," Nikolay replied. "Meanwhile," he said, addressing Rajesh, "please check the vegetable store. I think there is some issue with the temperature."

"Okay, Nikolay, I will check," Rajesh assured him, his mind turning to the technicalities of refrigeration systems and temperature controls.

The day began in earnest on-board the *MV Kurasova*, the sound of metal-to-metal de-rusting echoing across the deck as the crew set to work. The ship was a microcosm of the world, a miniature society where different nationalities—Indians, Sri Lankans, Burmese, Bulgarians, Ukrainians, and Filipinos—worked side by side in harmony. Each man had a role to play, and each took pride in ensuring that the ship's beauty never faded, her strength never faltered.

The clock turned quickly, and as the sun dipped below the horizon, casting long shadows across the deck, Bosun Lewis reported back to the chief officer. The day's tasks had been completed, the ship's maintenance was on track, and the crew, satisfied with their work, prepared for the evening. The *MV Kurasova* sailed on through the dark ocean, her crew united by their purpose and the silent bond of life at sea.

Chapter 8

Reminiscences on the Pacific

ODYSSEY
PACIFIC OCEAN

One week had passed since they cast off from the Yalappa Boat Club, their small yacht cutting through the waves of the vast Pacific Ocean. What began as a thrilling adventure, a quest to conquer the mighty Pacific, had slowly morphed into a monotonous routine. The initial surge of adrenaline that had filled their hearts was now tempered by the relentless, unchanging scenery—endless blue skies above and an even bluer sea below. The horizon, that thin line where sky and water met, seemed impossibly far, and no matter how far they sailed, it remained just as distant. Every direction was the same, a disorienting sameness that played tricks on the mind.

By night, the sky was a canopy of stars, each one a pinprick of light in the dark velvet above. The stars were their only companions, distant and indifferent to the tiny vessel below. It was under this starry sky that Christy and Willy found themselves talking about life, reminiscing about the years that had brought them to this point. They had been inseparable since childhood, their lives intertwined in ways that only decades of friendship could forge.

Christy was a man who had built his life from the ground up. He was a real estate lawyer, but not just any lawyer; he was one of the most expensive and successful in the city. His journey had not been easy. When he chose to specialize in real estate law, many of his peers had scoffed. Criminal law was where the glamor and money lay, they said. But Christy had seen something others hadn't, and with Willy by his side, he had persevered. Today, his law firm was a towering success, known for its integrity and its near-perfect record in court, and his name commanded respect in the industry.

As they sailed, Christy's mind often wandered back to the trials that awaited him once they reached home. His son, Robert, had been holding the fort in his absence, managing the law firm from the family's mansion. The mansion was not just a home; it was an institution, a place where law and life were inextricably linked. Robert and his wife, Sofia, lived there too, along with their daughter. Sofia was a lawyer by training, but she had never practiced. Instead, she had taken on the role of the firm's administrator, a role she excelled in. She had a sharp mind for business, and under her management, the firm had flourished even further.

However, not all memories were pleasant. The ocean, with its vastness, had a way of pulling buried memories to the surface, and Christy could not help but think of the day his life had changed forever—the day he lost his wife. Robert had been just eleven years old.

It had been a typical day, or so it seemed. Christy had left for work, Robert for school, and his wife had gone to take a shower after seeing them off. When Christy made his routine call home during lunch, there was no answer. At first, he thought nothing of it—perhaps she had gone out for a bit. But as the minutes ticked by, a sense of dread began to creep in. He called repeatedly, but still, no answer. Panic set in. He asked their aunt who stayed close by to check home if everything was okay. He sensed that something was wrong and raced home, his heart pounding with fear.

When he arrived, the scene that greeted him was one of horror. The police were already there, their faces grim. His wife had been found in the bathtub; her life drained away by her own hand. The water had turned red with blood, and her wrists bore the distinct signs of suicide. But the why of it all—why she had done it—remained a mystery. There had been no note, no warning, no sign that anything was wrong. It was as if she had simply slipped away, leaving behind only questions that would never be answered.

The loss had shattered Christy and Robert. In the days and weeks that followed, they had struggled to find a way to go on. It was Willy and his wife, Anna, who had stepped in, their support the lifeline that kept Christy and Robert from sinking into despair. Willy and Anna, both professors at the same university, had been close friends of the family for years. They had no children of their own, but they had always loved Robert as if he were their own. After the tragedy, Anna had given up her career to care for Robert, devoting herself to helping him heal.

As Robert grew older, the bond between him and Anna deepened. She became not just a guardian, but a second mother, guiding him through the darkest times. When Robert graduated, Anna returned to work, but not to the world of academia. Instead, she joined Christy's law firm, taking charge of its charitable initiatives. Anna had always had a strong sense of social responsibility, and in her new role, she found a way to channel that into something meaningful. She became a powerful advocate for children who had lost their mothers, creating programs and initiatives that changed lives. Her work earned her widespread respect, and in time, she became a beloved figure in the community.

Willy, meanwhile, had continued his academic career, rising through the ranks to become a senior professor. But even after he retired, his thirst for knowledge never faded. At the age of sixty-five, he surprised everyone by enrolling in law school, determined to join Christy's firm in a more meaningful way. It had been a challenge, but Willy was not a man to shy away from challenges. He graduated with honors, and now, he was an integral part of Christy's firm, bringing his unique perspective and wisdom to the table.

Then there was Juan, the quiet skipper who kept his thoughts to himself. He listened as Christy and Willy shared their stories, but he offered none of his own. Juan had spent his life at sea, a born sailor who had navigated the waters around Mexico for as long as he could remember. He was good at what he did, but it was a hard life, one that never quite brought in enough to secure a comfortable future for his family.

Ten days earlier, two mad elderly men had approached him in a nightclub near the Yalappa Boat Club. They were looking for a skipper for their new yacht, and Juan had seemed like the perfect candidate. It had sounded like just another job—until they told him their plan. They wanted to cross the Pacific Ocean, a journey that would take them from Mexico to New Zealand. Juan had laughed at the absurdity of it, then flatly refused. But the men were persistent. They tracked him down the next day and made him an offer that was impossible to refuse.

"You take us to Auckland, the other end of this ocean, then the *Odyssey* is yours"

They even promised to help him find a job in New Zealand to ensure that his family was taken care of. It was a dangerous gamble, but the stakes were too high to ignore. Juan had spent his life dreaming of a better future, and this might be his only chance to achieve it. So, he agreed.

Now, the three of them were alone in the ocean, their fates intertwined. The nights were long, the days longer, but together, they sailed on, driven by a shared determination to reach their destination. None of them had the faintest idea what their fates had in store for them.

Chapter 9

Drills and Duties on the MV Kurasova

Trrrrrr... Trrrrrr... Trrrrrr... The ship's horn blared sharply at 1500 hours. Instantly, every crew member dropped what they were doing and rushed to their muster stations. An emergency had been signaled, its nature unknown, and the ship's horn roared with an urgency that demanded immediate response. Within three minutes, the entire crew had assembled at their designated stations.

The chief officer, head of the emergency muster station, swiftly reported to the bridge, "All crew members present at the muster station. Head count taken. Waiting for instructions."

"Roger." The reply came from the command center.

"Gentlemen, this is a drill. I repeat, this is a drill," Captain Bijoy announced over the public address system.

The chief officer and the chief engineer were the only ones aware of the drill beforehand. By keeping the details of the training confidential, they ensured that the crew would be able to respond swiftly and efficiently at any moment, without prior warning.

The crew let out a collective sigh of relief; there was no emergency this time either.

No matter how seasoned and experienced a seafarer might be, the drills and training sessions were mandatory. Bijoy insisted on making these drills as realistic as possible. Such exercises were crucial in familiarizing the crew with the ship and its safety equipment. Upon joining the ship, each crew member's duties were meticulously recorded and explained to them and then followed up by routine training sessions.

"Gentlemen, smoke reported from the galley," the captain announced.

"Emergency team, prepare the firefighters and start boundary cooling. Do not enter until I give the command," He continued after a pause.

"Roger, command team," came the prompt response.

"Support team, prepare the first aid kit and ready the lifeboat for emergency."

"Roger, command team."

"Engine room team, prepare to slow down and cut all electric power to the galley."

"Roger, command team."

Captain Bijoy continued to issue instructions as the drill commenced. They simulated firefighting in the galley, each team performing their duties flawlessly, and within fifteen minutes, the drill was wrapped up. Captain Bijoy felt a surge of pride seeing his crew's efficient response. He and his team had worked diligently over the past four months to ensure that everyone was always prepared for emergencies.

A merchant ship was a world within a world, where a team of twenty-five crew members had to be ready for any contingency. The life and safety of everyone on-board were a collective responsibility.

The emergency alarm sounded again, signaling an abandon ship drill. The crew mustered once more. Chief Officer Gregory led the session. He inspected the life jackets of various crew members at random, ensuring they were in good condition and would function properly in an emergency. Then he demonstrated the lifeboat launching procedures in meticulous detail.

"Gentlemen, the lifeboat is designed so that if you are the sole survivor on-board during an emergency, you should be able to launch it to save your life," Gregory explained, his passion evident. At six foot four, with a strong build, Gregory's presence was commanding, and his explanations were often dramatic. In most ships, if a training session extended, the chief cook would be allowed to leave early. But with Gregory, every moment was an opportunity for thorough instruction.

Gregory's enthusiasm was contagious as he detailed the life-saving techniques. "Remember, gentlemen, the sea can be ruthless. Our readiness is our only safeguard. Each one of you must be able to rely on these drills, to know your role without hesitation." Although these topics had been addressed many times before, the repetition helped reinforce the information and ensure it was firmly registered in everyone's mind.

The training continued, and Gregory instructed Third Officer Andrei to explain the EPIRB (Emergency Position Indicating Radio Beacon) equipment. He wanted to check if the new third officer met their expectations. To his surprise, Andrei was quite excited by the opportunity to share his knowledge.

"Have you ever seen this equipment stored near the navigation bridge?" Andrei asked the crew, holding up the tiny device with a rat-tail-like antenna on its head.

Everyone raised their hands to show that they had seen it, as they had all been taken on a familiarization round after joining the ship.

"Do you know how to use it or how it works?"

This time, only a few senior sailors raised their hands.

"This is an emergency radio beacon that stores our ship's identity. In an emergency, we have to press this button to activate it. The EPIRB (he pronounced it 'e-purrb') will transmit our information and current location to a global Rescue Coordination Centre. The beacon operates via a satellite system: the signal is sent to a satellite, which then relays it to the rescue center. The rescue center will identify the ship in emergency and plot the position using GPS coordinates. This will help them to coordinate rescue operations by checking for any nearby ships."

Senior mariners stood as if they had heard it a thousand times. Many times, these training sessions were boring. However, it was compulsory to keep doing it.

"What if the rescue center or nearby ships don't come to help us?"

Everyone turned towards the direction of the voice, a fresh engine room trainee who had just joined.

"Everybody helps, because we are sailors at sea. Saving lives is our duty," Lewis, the bosun said firmly.

"And, we have an obligation by law to help fellow sailors, so there is no escape," Gregory added.

The training session continued, and the long hand of the ship's clock hit twelve while the short one pointed to six. Captain Bijoy advised Gregory to end the session because he knew his favorite Ukrainian brat would not stop until someone told him to.

Bosun Lewis and his team went back to secure their workspace while the others went for dinner. Another day ended at sea as the *MV Kurasova* cut through the surface of the mighty Pacific Ocean.

As the sun dipped below the horizon, painting the sky in shades of crimson and gold, the crew settled into the rhythms of the evening. Conversations floated around the mess hall, punctuated by laughter and the clinking of cutlery. The crew knew that their lives depended on each other's skills and knowledge, and that understanding forged a bond stronger than the steel of the ship.

In the gathering darkness, the ship continued its journey, cutting a steady path through the dark waters. Bijoy took a deep breath, feeling the cool sea breeze on his face. He thought about the training they had undergone that day and felt a sense of fullfilment. The trainings were not just about following regulations; they were about ensuring that, in the face of real danger, his crew could act swiftly and effectively. He was proud of his crew, proud of their dedication and their unwavering commitment to safety.

Within the heart of the ship, the hum of machinery blended with the soft murmur of conversations, creating a symphony of life at sea. Each crew member, from the seasoned mariners to the fresh trainees, was a vital part of this floating world.

Chapter 10

Of Bonds and Dreams

———— ◆◆◆ ————

"Yeah, Dad, I'll have the papers submitted by the end of tomorrow."

"Oh, and we've had both the clients approach us about settlements. That case will end soon. Sofia's handling it, so we'll have it sorted before you get back."

"She's in the kitchen right now; we're getting ready for dinner."

"Aunt Anna won't pick up the phone, I'm sure of it. Tell Uncle Willy to brace himself for a bit of a tussle with her once you're back."

"That's correct; it's pouring down here with heavy lightning and thunder. It's been going on for nearly four hours straight."

"Okay, Dad, talk to you tomorrow. You sound a bit worn out. Make sure to look after yourself. Love you heaps and see you soon."

Robert hung up the call from his father and walked back to the dining table, where his six-year-old daughter, Annette, was lost in the world of her drawing. Despite the heavy rain and the occasional flash of lightning, the gentle scratch of her crayon against the paper was a soothing contrast. Her yacht was a burst of color and joy, and the name written on it read 'ODYSSEY' with three figures aboard— one, Willy, sported a bushy moustache, the second, Christy, wore a cheerful striped sailor's shirt. Both were drawn with broad smiles that seemed to leap off the page. The third figure, whose face was still a blank canvas, was captured in a mid-playful gesture.

Robert, watching with a mixture of amusement and affection, could not resist teasing his daughter. "Annette, sweetheart, this is the seventh drawing you've made of your grandfather's yacht out at sea, and still no eyes, nose, or lips for Juan?" he asked, his tone light and playful.

Annette looked up from her work, her eyes wide with innocence. "I haven't seen him yet, Daddy. Once I see him, I'll fill in the blanks," she replied earnestly.

Robert chuckled, trying to playfully grab her crayon. "I heard your grandfather has grown his beard all the way down to his belly button in the last month."

Annette giggled and bolted towards the kitchen, where her mother, Sofia, and Robert's Aunt Anna were bustling about, preparing dinner. "I'll draw that too once they're back!" she said, hiding behind her mother, her laughter echoing through the house.

Robert helped set the dinner on the table when he noticed Anna's flushed face, clearly fuming.

"Aunty, Uncle Willy mentioned he bought some special red roses from Mexico just for you," Robert teased, trying to lighten the mood. Sofia could not stifle a laugh at the remark.

"Robert, don't start with me now," Anna snapped, her voice tinged with frustration. "Your uncle, my so-called beloved husband, hasn't bothered to call me since he left Mexico."

Robert, always affectionate, drew his aunt close and wrapped his arms around her from behind. "He did ask me to call you, but you were always so busy with your endless parade of motherless children. Are you still seeing me in them?" he said gently. To him, Anna was like a mother.

Anna shrugged him off with a dismissive nudge. "Robert, I have known you since you were a child, just like Annette. You can't lie to me; your eyes give you away."

"Then just divorce him as you always threaten to do," Sofia chimed in as they took their seats around the dinner table. "You'd find men lining up for you, Aunty. Just look at you—you're stunning."

Anna's gaze softened as she looked at Annette's drawing, her frustration still evident. "I don't mind, Sofia, but Willy wouldn't last a day without me. Sure, he was a big name at Auckland University with an impressive collection of research papers, but he cannot even find his own clothes in the closet. That is how careless he is. I'm sure Christy is managing everything on their mad trip, with Willy just following along like a baby duck trailing after its mother."

As they began their meal—Sofia and Annette enjoying mashed potatoes and grilled chicken breast, while Robert and Anna settled on a light kiwi-cucumber salad—Anna continued, her voice carrying a mix of exasperation and affection. "He's just a grown-up boy. Too careless to even call his wife to say hello. Wherever he is, he's as distant as ever."

"Leave it, Aunty. Just three more days and they will be here. We'll make their arrival a big event—probably the first Kiwis to cross the Pacific in a yacht," Sofia said while helping Annette slice her chicken breast.

Anna sighed; her concern palpable. "I'm just praying, sweetheart. Spending time on a restless trip through South America was one thing, but crossing the ocean in a boat? What madness! They never even mentioned this to me earlier. I wouldn't have agreed to it."

Sofia noticed a subtle shift in Robert's expression. She could tell from the slight change in his face that he was also deeply worried about his father and uncle's adventurous sail from Mexico to Auckland. Though he rarely spoke of it, these small, telling changes in his demeanor spoke volumes, understood only by those who truly knew and cared for him. She quickly shifted the conversation.

"Robert, that land settlement case might take a while. I just realized that the local body has a right over the property."

"Now that's a twist," Robert said, his surprise evident. "How bad is it? Dad just asked me about it."

"I've scheduled a meeting with both clients and a government representative tomorrow at noon. Hopefully, we can resolve it then," Sofia replied.

"Looks like your week's taking off with a busy schedule," Robert said.

"Let me know if you need any help," Anna offered, taking a bite of kiwifruit. "I'm familiar with the property and the people involved." As a social worker with strong connections, she was always a valuable resource.

"Daddy, what's Juan's daughter's name?" Annette asked, her mind wandering to her own playful thoughts.

"I don't know, sweetie. We'll ask your grandfather when he calls tomorrow," Robert replied.

"Will she play with me? She's also six," Annette persisted, not entirely satisfied with the answer.

"Of course, she will play with you. She'll be your best friend," Anna assured her.

"Robert, what's your father's plan for Juan and his family? Is he still set on bringing them to New Zealand? Remember, it'll be a lot of paperwork for Mexican emigrants," Anna inquired.

"I talked to the Auckland Boat Club about Juan. They're okay with offering him a job as a skipper on their leisure yachts that cruise around New Zealand," Robert said.

"The family probably won't move until after three months, which is how long we expect the paperwork to take," Sofia added.

"Another wild idea from these old men, bringing over another family. Mad people," Anna said with a laugh. Robert and Sofia joined in, their laughter lightening the mood. Meanwhile, Annette began drawing a picture of two six-year-old girls playing with a teddy bear.

As they finished dinner and prepared for bed, the rain outside pounded against the windows with a relentless, rhythmic drumbeat. Jagged flashes of lightning intermittently illuminated the mansion, standing firm like a fortress, while the thunder rumbled and shook the very walls.

Chapter 11

Sunday Traditions

MV KURASOVA
PACIFIC OCEAN
SUNDAY

Sunday on the open sea was the perfect backdrop for the ship's crew to unwind and take a break from their demanding routines. While the watch keepers stayed on duty, the rest of the crew enjoyed beer, movies, and sports. Chief Engineer Rajesh Kumar took charge of organizing the cricket matches, while Rizilino, a Filipino crew member, managed the basketball games. They made sure that the activities started promptly after breakfast and continued until lunchtime.

Sundays were a celebration, marked by the fragrant aroma of biryani and the clinking of beer bottles in the mess rooms, where lunch often stretched until three in the afternoon. The afternoons on-board were a delight, filled with karaoke and musical performances by the talented Filipino crew members.

The atmosphere during these long voyages was always special, a blend of camaraderie and routine that kept spirits high.

Captain Bijoy approached his Sundays with a sense of duty. Mornings were reserved for pending paperwork, weekly reports, plans for the next week, inspections, etc.—a task he undertook with unwavering dedication until 1100 hours. Once his paperwork was completed, he conducted the weekly accommodation inspection, accompanied by senior officers and the bosun. This meticulous routine ensured the ship remained in pristine condition, with every corner checked for cleanliness and hygiene. Rajesh, however, would often skip this session, his heart and mind firmly anchored to the cricket pitch.

As evening approached, preparations for weekly movie night began for Bijoy. Wine was uncorked, and the chosen film was always the same: *Top Gun*. This iconic action drama, featuring Tom Cruise as the fearless fighter pilot, Maverick, held a special place in his heart. His father, an air force pilot, had died in combat when Bijoy was just a schoolboy. Watching *Top Gun* was a bittersweet ritual, a way to honor his father's memory. With the Italian wine set on the table, Bijoy paused the movie to attend to his duties on the navigation bridge. It was 2030 hours, and Third Officer Andrei was on duty.

"Hi, Third, how's everything?" Captain Bijoy inquired.

"Good evening, Captain. All good. No traffic, slight drizzle outside, and the temperature is less than four degrees," Andrei reported.

"Oh, that's bad. This bloody drizzle can kill the mood," Bijoy muttered, studying the radar screen. It was clear, no targets around. The radar scanner continued its rhythmic turns. He then moved to the chart table, where the night order book awaited. The night orders would speak for him until morning, during his slumber.

Bijoy took out his golden pen, a treasured gift from a former captain under whom he had served as a trainee cadet. He meticulously noted all the key points in the night orders: expected weather, the speed the vessel should maintain at night, instructions for night patrolling, and finally, he signed off and capped the pen with his most important remark:

"Do not hesitate to call me for any doubts, or at six in the morning, whichever is deemed necessary."

A thorough scan of the bridge and its navigation equipment followed. He was beginning to trust Andrei, despite the third officer's occasional absent-mindedness in conversation.

"Third, as usual, read and sign the night orders. I know the traffic is almost nil, but do not be carried away. Do not do any paperwork while you're on duty. Call me if you have even the slightest doubt," Bijoy instructed firmly.

"Yes, Captain," Andrei nodded.

"Okay, gentlemen, have a good watch."

"Good night, Captain."

Bijoy descended the stairs to his cabin, the distant chatter and laughter of the crew still audible. Bosun Lewis's boisterous laughter echoed through the corridors, promising a lively evening until at least nine. In the alleyway, Bijoy encountered Rajesh. As usual, their conversation revolved around family and cricket. Bijoy often marvelled at how Rajesh's wife, a stern college lecturer, tolerated his cricket obsession.

Finally, upon reaching his cabin, he found Second Officer Amol waiting with a stack of papers needing signatures. He invited Amol in, settled into his chair, and resumed watching the movie, deftly signing the documents as he did so.

As another Sunday wound down on-board the MV Kuras*ova*, the ocean stretched endlessly before them, the horizon swallowed by an infinite expanse. The sound of waves parting for the mighty vessel was a constant, rhythmic pulse, while a breath-taking array of jellyfish illuminated the water ahead with an ethereal green glow, casting an enchanting, otherworldly light against the gathering darkness.

Chapter 12

Trouble in Paradise

ODYSSEY
PACIFIC OCEAN
TIME: 0030 HOURS
MONDAY

Christy stood alone on the deck, his eyes scanning the endless expanse of the Pacific. The *Odyssey* moved steadily forward, its sails catching the cool night breeze as the stars twinkled like distant beacons above. He was the night watchman for the day, entrusted with the responsibility of guiding them safely through the dark hours, while Willy and Juan rested below deck.

His thoughts drifted to the celebration awaiting them in Auckland. It would be a grand occasion where two national heroes, and their revered Mexican skipper, would be honored by their families. Less than eighty hours separated them from that momentous event. Tomorrow, they would spot the first signs of land. The birds that would be their initial greeters, heralding the end of their long journey. The idea of stepping onto solid ground, surrounded by loved ones and basking in their accolades, filled him with a quiet anticipation. But tonight, as the yacht cruised serenely on autopilot, there was an undercurrent of unease that Christy couldn't shake off.

The gentle rhythm of the waves lapping against the hull, the soft rustle of the sails, and the distant hum of the autopilot were all familiar sounds, yet they seemed to blend into a discordant symphony that set his nerves on edge. His senses picked up something out of place. It was subtle at first—a faint, almost imperceptible scent carried by the wind. However, as it grew stronger, Christy's heart began to pound.

It was the smell of oil.

In an instant, Christy was yanked out of his thoughts. The sweet, cloying scent of oil, out of place in the crisp, salty air, became more pronounced, mingling with the night breeze. His eyes darted to the engine room door, which was slightly ajar. A chill ran down his spine, his instincts screaming that something was terribly wrong.

His pulse quickened, and adrenaline coursed through his veins, sharpening his focus. The distant twinkling of the stars, the peaceful expanse of the ocean, all faded into the background as his mind raced through the possibilities. He could feel the blood pounding in his ears as he took a cautious step toward the engine room. His breath came in short, shallow bursts, the anxiety gnawing at him with every passing second.

The smell of oil grew stronger, almost tangible now, as if the air itself was thick with it. Christy reached the engine room door, his hand trembling as he grasped the metal handle. He hesitated, memories flashing before his eyes—voyages taken, miles weathered, the faces of loved ones waiting in Auckland, the promise of a hero's welcome. But this was no time for reminiscences or hesitation.

He pulled open the door, and the heat hit him like a physical force. Flames leaped out, wild and untamed, consuming everything in their path. The roar of the fire was deafening, drowning out the steady hum of the autopilot and the gentle lapping of the waves. Panic surged through Christy, but he fought it down.

"Fire! Fire! Fire!" he shouted, his voice cutting through the tranquil night, urgent and piercing.

Below deck, Willy and Juan jolted awake, the urgency in Christy's voice shattering the peace of their slumber.

In an instant, they were on their feet, adrenaline banishing the last remnants of sleep.

"Grab the extinguishers!" Juan's voice rang out with commanding urgency as he sprinted toward the emergency equipment. He wrenched open the engine room hatch, and his heart sank at the sight that met him: amber flames leaped viciously, consuming the engine in their fiery jaws. A fleeting thought crossed his mind about the repair he had done on the main engine fuel oil pipe just days ago. *Damn it, this is not the time for that.* The fire was spreading rapidly, the heat was suffocating, and the air was thick with choking smoke.

Juan had seen enough to know that they were out of time. The yacht was a ticking time bomb, the fire threatening to reach the fuel tanks at any moment. There was no time to think, only to act.

"We have to abandon the boat immediately," Juan commanded, his voice steady despite the chaos. He moved to the life raft, his hands moving with precision as he unlocked it and pushed it into the sea. "The yacht won't survive the fire."

Christy and Willy exchanged a quick glance, their expressions grim but resolute. There was no time for questions, no room for doubt. They trusted Juan's seasoned judgment implicitly.

They grabbed the life jackets stored beneath the chart table and donned them swiftly, each second ticking away with increasing urgency. The calm, steady rhythm of their voyage was now a distant memory, overshadowed by the frantic urgency of survival.

"Take the EPIRB," Juan instructed, his voice straining as he yanked the rope to deploy the life raft.

Willy grabbed the EPIRB almost mechanically, securing it around his neck. The life raft began to inflate with a loud hiss, expanding into a fragile bubble of safety amidst the chaos.

With the life raft fully inflated, Juan shoved Christy and Willy into it, securing their fragile haven to the yacht. Flames roared from the engine room, thick black smoke billowing into the night sky. However, as Juan turned back, a thought crossed his mind – a fleeting, foolish thought, but one he could not ignore.

The black-and-white photo of his family, the one he had kept by the steering wheel for the entire journey, it was a symbol of his purpose, a reminder of why he was out here in the first place. Without thinking, he dashed back, desperate to retrieve it. Nevertheless, in that moment, the *Odyssey*, already pushed to her limits, could take no more.

A deafening explosion tore through the air, the force of it throwing Juan off his feet. The metal door of the engine room flew off its hinges, striking Juan with brutal force and sending him sprawling onto the deck. The photo, his precious keepsake, shattered on impact, the glass fragments scattering across the deck as he was hurled into the water.

He fell just behind the yacht, the cold, dark water swallowing him up. The last thing he saw before everything went black was the shattered remains of his family photo; the last sound, the explosion that had sealed their fate.

"Juan, Juan…" The voice pierced through the fog that clouded his mind. He struggled to open his eyes, pain searing through his body. His right leg felt like it was on fire.

"Juan, don't worry. You're in the life raft," Willy said, his voice steady but laced with concern.

Juan's throat was dry, his mind struggling to make sense of what had happened.

"We lost the *Odyssey*," Willy continued, his words blunt but necessary. "There was a massive explosion when you were on deck. A metal plank hit your leg and threw you into the water. There's swelling, but we managed to get you into the raft."

Slowly, the fog lifted, and Juan's mind cleared. The weight of their situation settled over him like a heavy shroud. The *Odyssey*—the yacht they had sailed—was gone, reduced to debris scattered across the ocean. Clad in nothing but life jackets, they were adrift under the starry canopy in a two-meter life raft, surrounded by the vast, indifferent sea. Images of possible demise—ten different ways to die out here in the open ocean—flashed through Juan's mind, each more terrifying than the previous one.

But he couldn't afford to succumb to fear. Christy and Willy looked at him with desperate hope, their eyes mirroring a shared determination. Three families awaited their return on opposite shores of the Pacific Ocean. Failure was not an option. Juan was a proud sailor, born to be one of the unsung heroes of the sea. The sea had taught him resilience and the importance of swift, decisive action.

With grim determination, Juan grabbed the EPIRB from Willy's neck and activated it, his eyes closing as a silent prayer escaped his lips. As the signal was sent out into the void, the three men huddled together in their fragile raft, each one clinging to the hope that rescue would come before the ocean claimed them.

Chapter 13

An Urgent Mission

At 1800 hours, the evening began with the usual lazy European drizzle. A dull climate pervaded the atmosphere, accompanied by the gentle rustling of green leaves in the light breeze. Outside a pristine white building, five cars were parked neatly in a row, their windshields speckled with droplets of rain. The sign above the entrance read: Mission Rescue Coordination Centre (MRCC).

Inside, the building was a hive of specialized activity, divided into five distinct rooms, each dedicated to different duties and departments. Station No. 3, the nerve center of operations, was a large, high-tech room that hummed with the low buzz of electronic equipment. Rows of LED screens, each one depicting different segments of the world's oceans, cast a bluish glow across the space, creating an almost otherworldly atmosphere.

Emma and Alder stood beside the coffee machine, filling their mugs with the steaming liquid that would fuel them through the initial hours of their shift. Emma, in particular, clung to her custom-made Byrne Munich mug. Alder, on the other hand, wore a light smile as he stirred his espresso, his eyes twinkling with a hint of mischief. Emma tried to ignore him.

"Hey, Emma, what's up?" Alder began, his voice carrying that playful tone she had come to expect.

"Look, Alder, I'm not interested in talking if you're trying to pull my leg about last night's football match," Emma said, folding her arms across her chest, her expression stern.

Everyone at the MRCC knew that Emma Schuler was a die-hard Bayern Munich fan. She never missed a match, and unfortunately, her beloved team had suffered a humiliating 4-0 defeat the previous night. Although Alder was not much into football, he never missed the chance to tease Emma about her team's performance. They had been working the same shift for the past eight months, and this dynamic had become a familiar part of their routine.

"That's okay, Emma. I just wonder how they could lose so badly," Alder remarked, his grin widening.

"Oh no, Alder. One defeat does not make the club any worse. It was not an important match, so we rested our main players. They just played for fun. We fans won't even consider this match as one of ours," Emma retorted, her tone defensive.

Alder chuckled, adjusting his glasses as he tried to contain his laughter.

"Come on, let's get to work," Emma said, eager to change the subject and escape the teasing.

"Yes, we should. But first, a quick match analysis," Alder quipped, still grinning.

Emma's face flushed with irritation, but as she opened her mouth to retort, a piercing alarm sounded, cutting through their banter. A red spot began blinking urgently on one of the enormous screens. The shift from casual conversation to professional urgency was immediate. They both abandoned their coffee mugs and rushed to the main console.

The screen displayed a section of the Pacific Ocean. An EPIRB signal was flashing. Emma tapped the LED touch display, and a detailed information box popped up.

"*Odyssey*," they both read aloud, their expressions growing serious.

An EPIRB alert could signify a life-or-death situation or could prove to be a false alarm, but they could not afford to take any chances as long as life was involved. Alder grabbed the mouthpiece of the Public Address System.

"Attention all stations, attention all stations. Emergency, code red. Proceed to station number three immediately," he announced, his voice echoing through the center. This call to action summoned other teams, including the operation commanders, to their station.

Emma was already digging through the database for more information on the *Odyssey* gathering key details about the vessel and even securing its satellite phone number. Within moments, the other seven members of the station arrived, and Commander Bernard took the helm of the situation. Emma quickly briefed him.

"Sir, we have received an EPIRB alert from coordinates 21-30S, 169-03W. The vessel is named *Odyssey*, a

17-meter-long and 5-meter-wide pleasure craft. I have tried contacting the craft via satellite phone multiple times, but there is no response. I'm afraid the craft might be lost," she reported, her voice steady despite the gravity of the situation.

"Alright," Bernard responded, his expression grim. "Where is it registered? Pass me the owner information."

Alder sifted through the database and retrieved the required information. "The boat is registered to an owner from New Zealand, and the purchase was made just two weeks ago," he said, handing Bernard the contact details. The commander dialed the number, the seconds stretching as the call connected across the globe.

The phone buzzed sharply on the bedside table on the other side of the planet, its vibration slicing through the rain-soaked night in Auckland. Robert, Sofia, and their daughter were cocooned in deep sleep. For a fleeting second, the vibration melded with the rain, almost lulling Robert further into the warmth of his bed. Finally, the realization hit him: it was a phone call. With a sense of foreboding creeping into his half-asleep mind, Robert stretched out his hand, groping blindly for the phone. His eyes remained shut, but his pulse quickened as his fingers closed around the device. Robert was not accustomed to late-night calls from his workplace; a call at this hour was unusual and alarming.

"Yes, Robert here," answered a voice, groggy from sleep.

"Hello, Robert. I am Bernard from the Maritime Rescue Coordination Centre in Germany. Are you the owner of a vessel named the *Odyssey*?" Bernard asked, his tone professional and direct.

"No, that's my father, Christabel. What happened? Is everything okay?" Robert responded, his concern immediately evident. He slipped out of bed, careful not to wake his wife and daughter, and moved to the living room. The urgency in Bernard's voice was unmistakable, and Robert's mind raced with possibilities.

"We've received a distress alert from the Pacific Ocean from the *Odyssey* about ten minutes ago. We're unable to make contact with it via satellite phone," Bernard explained.

"How is that possible? I talked to my father just three hours ago. They are supposed to arrive in three days," Robert said, his voice rising with anxiety.

"We're gathering more information and will update you as soon as we can," Bernard assured him before ending the call.

Robert stared at the cordless receiver in his hand, his mind numb with fear. He wanted desperately to believe that this was just a nightmare. He opened the bedroom door slightly and saw his wife, Sofia, and their daughter sleeping soundly. Closing the door quietly, he sank onto the sofa, repeatedly dialling the *Odyssey*'s number without any success.

Back at the MRCC, Alder and Emma worked swiftly to identify any vessels in the vicinity of the distress signal's coordinates. Zooming in on the screen, they spotted a green triangular icon – a vessel with an active AIS (Automatic Identification System).

"Sir, we have one vessel close to the reported position," Alder announced, his voice cutting through the tension.

"How far?" Bernard asked, his eyes fixed on the screen.

"Eighteen nautical miles," Alder replied.

"Holy God, those damn fools in the *Odyssey* might be lucky, if they are alive," Bernard muttered, a glimmer of hope in his voice.

"Folks, this is going to be a long evening, so get ready," he continued.

Emma tapped on the triangular icon, and a new window displayed the ship's details. Everyone read out the name aloud:

"Container ship *MV Kurasova*."

Chapter 14

An Unexpected Message

MV KURASOVA
PACIFIC OCEAN
TIME: 0040 HOURS
MONDAY

It was forty minutes past midnight when Second Officer Amol finally reached the bridge for his navigational watch. He was forty minutes late. An unusual lapse in his otherwise disciplined routine. The events of the previous night had taken an unexpected turn. Instead of heading straight to his cabin after dinner, as was his custom, he found himself in the captain's cabin, delivering the usual paperwork for the medical logbook. What should have been a brief exchange turned into an evening of camaraderie, a shared bottle of wine, and a movie watched in easy companionship. By the time Amol finally retired to his cabin, it was well past 2230 hours, much later than his usual sleeping time.

The indulgences of the evening had taken their toll on him. The wine, coupled with the lateness of the hour, ensured that his sleep was deep, undisturbed, and, unfortunately, oblivious to his alarm. It wasn't until the third officer's wake-up call jolted him from his slumber that he realized he had overslept. A cold wave of panic hit him as he wiped the dried saliva from his cheek.

Amol leaped from his bunk, his heart pounding. A quick glance at the clock confirmed his worst fear: 0030 hours. In a frenzy, he splashed cold water on his face, dressed with military precision, and bolted down the narrow, dimly lit corridors of the ship. The gentle sway of the vessel under the moonlit sky was in stark contrast to the urgency driving him forward.

"Sorry, Andrei, I overslept," Amol admitted, slightly breathless as he finally stepped onto the navigation bridge.

"No worries, Amol," Andrei replied with a reassuring smile. "The captain called about half an hour ago. Said to wake him if you didn't show up."

"Thanks, mate. Anything in the night orders or traffic to watch out for?" Amol asked, already scanning the instruments.

"Nothing major. Visibility is low due to the drizzle, and it is bloody freezing," Andrei said with a shrug.

The handover was smooth, punctuated by the usual exchange of information. Ten minutes later, Amol was fully up to speed, ready to assume his duty.

"Alright, Third, have a good night. Apologies again for being late," Amol said as Andrei made his way out.

"Don't sweat it. Have a good watch," Andrei replied, disappearing into the shadows of the ship's passageways.

Amol turned to the coffee machine, craving something strong to kickstart his watch. "Raja, have you had your coffee yet? Shall I make you one?" he asked the duty seaman.

"Yes, Second, I finished my coffee," came the prompt reply from Rajapakse Damitha Bimsara. Rajapakse— Raja for short—was the Sri Lankan lookout who would stand by Amol's side for the next four hours.

"I don't see any traffic on the radar, and the course is set for the next few hours. But keep a sharp lookout and report anything, no matter how small," Amol instructed, his tone authoritative, yet calm.

They settled into the watch, exchanging light banter, plotting the ship's position, and vigilantly scanning the horizon. An hour into the watch, Amol took a brief respite to make a celestial calculation, confirming the ship's position with the GPS. The stars had always fascinated him. To Amol, celestial navigation was not just a skill; it was a dialogue with the universe. He could lose himself in the simplicity and precision of it, feeling a deep satisfaction every time the sextant's readings matched the GPS coordinates.

The hours ticked by, the sea stretching endlessly before them, void of any traffic—a night that promised little excitement. As the clock struck 0230, Amol picked up the phone and dialled the engine room. It was a nightly ritual, an unspoken agreement between him and Third Engineer Rohit. Both on the same duty shift, they would check in at the same time, sharing a few moments of conversation to break the monotony.

"Hey, Rohit, what's up, buddy?" Amol asked.

"Nothing much, as usual. Three days to Auckland. What's the plan?"

"Some pubs, nothing else," replied Amol.

"Oh no, is it Catherine this time as well?" Rohit asked, fishing for something.

"Hey, no. That was done and dusted. She's not my type, buddy," Amol said, his tone mischievous.

"Really? It took four months to understand that?" Rohit teased him.

"Ha ha, leave that. How's your 'future boss' doing back home? Got everything ready for the big day?" Amol teased back, reminding Rohit about his upcoming wedding.

"She is good, a typical Montessori teacher. She can unearth all my secrets in just a few conversations," Rohit said, chuckling.

"Obviously, dude," you are just a kiddo with massive muscles!" Amol said and laughed.

"Shall we go for skydiving this time?" Rohit, the Mad Max of *MV Kurasova*, asked.

"I would love to. But it will take time. I don't think we will have that much time since the Captain is signing off."

"Then let's at least do a bungee jump at the Auckland Sky Tower. The tallest in the Southern Hemisphere."

"That will be fun. Let's plan it."

Beep… Beep… Beep… Beep. The electronic alarm emitted a sharp chirp from the right corner, prompting Rohit and Raja to turn their heads in its direction.

"Rohit, I will call you back. I am receiving a satellite message," Amol said, looking at the small communication center on the navigation bridge.

Amol moved to the communications desk and shut off the alarm. The automatic printer came to life and began printing out a message. His eyes scanned the position coordinates on the printout. They seemed strangely familiar. He ripped the message from the printer and flipped open the logbook, his fingers tracing the coordinates he had recorded just half an hour earlier. A frown creased his forehead as he compared the coordinates.

Chapter 15

Mounting the Rescue Mission

"Raja, keep a sharp lookout. I will be inside," Amol said, rushing to the chart room.

"Okay, Sir," Raja responded, his tone clipped and professional.

Amol tightened his grip on the printed message as he entered the chart room. He turned up the yellow light and scanned the urgent message. His heart pounded, each beat amplified by the weight of responsibility.

From: The Maritime Rescue Mission Centre, Germany

To: The Master, MV Kurasova

Distress Position: 21-30S 169-03W

Vessel Name: Odyssey

We have received a distress alert via EPIRB from the above position. Your ship is in close vicinity. Request immediate assistance.

Amol's breath quickened as he grabbed the parallel ruler, his fingers moving with the precision of a seasoned navigator. In a few swift motions, he plotted the position on the chart, circling it with the pencil – a beacon of urgency amidst the calm, calculated lines of their planned course. Measuring the distance with a divider, his lips moved unconsciously.

"Eighteen miles… Oh my holy God," he whispered, the reality sinking in.

Wasting no time, Amol dialed 100 on the emergency telephone, the direct line to the captain's cabin. The line clicked open almost immediately.

"Yes, Captain speaking," came Bijoy's voice, crisp and alert, despite the late hour.

"Sir, emergency," Amol's voice was taut, the tension seeping through each word.

"Is my ship safe?" The captain's first instinct, as always, was the well-being of his vessel.

"Yes, Captain."

"Okay, I'm on my way."

Captain Bijoy arrived on the bridge within two minutes, his presence filling the space with an air of authority. The man had come straight from his bed, yet he exuded the readiness of a soldier in battle.

"Yes, Second, I'm listening," he said, his voice calm but laced with urgency. The situation had completely changed from when the second officer and the captain met just a couple of hours earlier.

"Sir, we received an emergency alert from the MRCC in Germany. I've plotted the position; it is eighteen nautical miles from us."

"Damn close," Bijoy muttered, checking the position marked on the chart paper. "Any navigational restrictions?"

"Negative, all clear, and no vessels nearby."

"Weather?"

"Drizzling, cold, with visibility around ten nautical miles."

Captain Bijoy bent over the chart, carefully measuring the distress position with his divider. He placed the tool on the table with precision and folded his arms across his chest. The bridge was enveloped in tense silence as he immersed himself in his calculations. Moments later, he reached a decision, his instincts honed by years at sea.

"Okay, let's proceed to the position. Raja, take the wheel and hard to starboard," he commanded, the resolute authority in his voice galvanizing the crew into action. "Inform the engine room I will need full speed."

"Eighteen nautical miles. We can reach it in about an hour and fifteen minutes."

"Yes, Captain," Amol replied, his voice steady as he relayed the orders to the engine room. Third Engineer Rohit was briefed in swift, clear terms; additional generators were fired up in anticipation of the speed increase.

The captain settled into the high chair in the radio room and typed a brief response:

"Well noted, we are proceeding to the distress position."

With a click, he sent the message, acknowledging receipt and confirming their course of action to the MRCC.

"Second, call the junior officer and an additional lookout to the bridge," the Captain instructed, his mind already calculating the next steps. "We'll need extra eyes on this."

"Roger Captain", Amol responded.

He stood near the navigation bridge window, mentally calculating and strategizing. Meanwhile, Amol was busy recording and carrying out the captain's orders.

'Hey, Captain, what's happening? Are we on a rescue mission?' Rajesh asked, stepping onto the bridge, his expression a mix of curiosity and concern, having been briefed by Rohit, the third engineer.

"Hi, Chief. We received a distress alert from the MRCC. It's about eighteen nautical miles from us. We're proceeding to the location now," Bijoy replied.

"All right, I will head to the engine room. Call me if you need any assistance," Rajesh responded, his tone reflecting the seriousness of the situation before he exited the bridge.

As the minutes ticked by, the tension on the bridge mounted. The steady beep of the satellite printer suddenly pierced the air, drawing every eye. Captain

Bijoy moved quickly, snatching the new printout. The distress position had shifted—four miles away from the original coordinates. A strong drift. With every passing minute, the search was becoming increasingly more difficult.

The bosun and an additional sailor arrived on the bridge. Lewis, sensing something amiss with the engine's pace even while asleep, had rushed to the bridge to investigate. A junior officer, having completed a full round of lookout, reported back to the captain.

"Sir, could it be a false alert? Since it's an EPIRB signal," the junior officer asked, his voice betraying a hint of doubt.

Captain Bijoy's response was immediate, his tone leaving no room for ambiguity. "It doesn't matter. Unless we have solid evidence that it is a false alert, we must assume someone is out there, in the deep black ocean, waiting for us. Perhaps we are destined to help them."

The bridge was a hive of activity, every crew member focused on the task at hand. Lewis, a veteran with years of seafaring experience behind him, barked orders for additional sailors, while Rajesh, ever vigilant, sent three more engine crew members to the bridge, ensuring they were prepared for anything.

"*ODYSSEY, ODYSSEY, ODYSSEY…* can you hear me?" Amol's voice resounded over the VHF radio, the repeated hailing becoming a grim mantra.

Six nautical miles from the distress position, and still, the horizon remained an unbroken line of gray. The drizzle, now turned into a relentless downpour, pelted the ship like icy needles, seeping through layers of clothing and biting into their skin. The weight of the unknown pressed down on them as they battled the elements, trying desperately to catch a glimpse of the stranded seafarers.

Chapter 16

Will We Survive?

———◆———

It had been nearly two hours since they activated the EPIRB, their last hope of sending a distress signal to the world beyond the endless horizon. Yet, they knew all too well that the equipment would not give them any acknowledgment, no reassuring beep or light to confirm that their signal had been received. Uncertainty gnawed at their nerves, leaving them with nothing but their prayers to cling to. They had all the distress flares at hand, and Christy, in his desperation, was eager to use them. However, Juan held him back. He knew the futility of sending out flares into the empty darkness of the ocean unless there was a chance—however slim—that another vessel might be close enough to see them.

The sea had changed. Its voice was no longer the rhythmic, almost comforting sound that they had grown accustomed to during their voyage. Now, it howled, a mournful wail that carried with it the cold, crippling sense of fear. The wind seemed to cut through the night, a relentless force that churned the black waves and sent them crashing against the frail sides of their life raft. Above, the sky was a menacing shade of pitch, as if the heavens themselves were cloaked in dread. A light drizzle began to fall, adding to the misery.

Christy and Willy clung to their belief in survival, their minds unwilling to accept any other outcome. They were men of faith, but Juan knew better. He understood the ocean, knew its unforgiving nature. The life raft, with one of its air chambers damaged in the explosion a couple of hours back, was a fragile shell, barely holding together. It was a desperate lifeline, nothing more than a two-meter speck in the vastness of the Pacific Ocean, carrying three souls who now teetered on the edge of oblivion.

Time dragged on, and with each passing minute, hope began to slip away. The reality of their situation settled over them like a shroud. Juan could feel the sharp, relentless pain in his right leg, broken in the explosion that had sent them fleeing from the yacht. But he fought to keep his composure, to be the rock that Christy and Willy needed him to be. He forced a smile, even as his body betrayed him. He made sure their life jackets were securely fastened, and despite the agony, he handed them anti-seasickness pills from the life raft's emergency pouch. Every action was deliberate, every movement an attempt to maintain a semblance of control.

As the hours passed, the thought of death loomed larger. The life raft listed slightly to one side, the damaged air chamber making its presence felt with every uncomfortable jolt as they were tossed about by the restless sea.

"Juan," Christy's voice broke the heavy silence, his trembling tone betraying his fear. "Will we see Robert again?" His hand gripped Willy's so tightly that his knuckles turned white.

Juan nodded, unable to meet Christy's gaze, and then looked away, his eyes scanning the darkness, searching for anything—anything at all—that might bring them hope.

Chapter 17

A Needle in a Haystack

"Call the Chief Officer," Bijoy ordered, his eyes never leaving the radar.

Amol dialled Gregory as they inched close to the distress location.

Chief Officer Gregory arrived on the bridge within minutes. As Bijoy quickly briefed him, Gregory's eyes narrowed, absorbing the gravity of the situation. The captain's concise update conveyed the urgency and seriousness of their mission, leaving no room for doubt.

"Captain, let us call all the crew to action," he suggested.

"Exactly, Chief," Bijoy responded and, in one swift motion, activated the emergency alarm.

Gregory dashed to the muster station. The ship's alarm system blared insistently, piercing through the deep slumber of the crew who had been enjoying a well-deserved rest after Sunday's celebrations. The sudden, relentless wail of the alarm jolted them awake, shattering their tranquillity. Groggy but alert, they rushed to the muster station.

At the muster station, Gregory took charge with unwavering determination. His voice cut through the clamour as he began to organize the crew, issuing clear and precise instructions. The crew members, many still in their sleepwear and rubbing the remnants of dreams from their eyes, exchanged brief, concerned glances.

"Command station, all crew present except the lookout on the bridge and three members in the engine room. Awaiting your orders," Chief Officer Gregory reported, his tone crisp and devoid of any hesitation.

"Roger, Emergency station. Prepare the lifeboat for launch," Bijoy commanded, his voice a steely reminder of the stakes at hand.

"Captain, will it be safe to launch the lifeboat in this weather?" Gregory asked, his concern for the crew evident, but his resolve unwavering.

"Yes, Chief. If we have to do it, then we will do it." There were no doubts in the captain's voice.

'Noted,' Gregory turned to the assembled crew, his face set in a mask of determination. 'Once you've prepared the lifeboat, I want all other crew members positioned on deck at different locations. Keep a very sharp lookout all around you.'

The crew moved with purpose, each member taking their place, their minds focused on the grim reality that awaited them. The lifeboat was prepared, and the third officer stood by, ready for whatever orders came next. From their vantage points along the ship, the crew scanned the horizon, eyes straining against the inky blackness of the night.

"Dead slow ahead," Bijoy ordered, his voice steady as the ship's speed decreased. Navigating through the modest waves at reduced speeds required skill, and the crew's resolve was tested as the drizzle turned into a biting cold downpour, stinging their faces like needles.

Lewis moved along the main deck, his hands working the ropes with the confidence of years at sea as a sailor. Despite the weather, he prepared for the worst, his mind focused on the task at hand. This was his first rescue mission in the thirty-five years of his career.

As the ship closed in on the distress position, the powerful searchlights on the bridge wings cut through the darkness, their beams sweeping across the churning sea. The ship's whistle blew incessantly, a relentless cry that echoed through the night. For the crew at the bow, it was a test of endurance, the spray from each wave drenching them, but they stood firm, eyes searching the void for any sign of life.

Twenty minutes passed, the tension on the bridge growing with each tick of the clock. Every wave that struck the vessel seemed to mock their efforts, the water spraying across the deck as if the ocean itself was resisting their rescue attempt. The ship moved with a measured, deliberate pace, each crew member on high alert, scanning the horizon with a mix of hope and dread.

"Sir, shall we inform the MRCC and stop the search?" Andrei asked, his voice tinged with the doubt that had been gnawing at him. The third officer had taken over the bridge duties from the second officer, who was now on deck assisting the chief officer.

Captain Bijoy did not respond immediately. Instead, he moved to the edge of the bridge, his eyes narrowing as he stared into the ocean. His mind raced, weighing every possibility, every protocol, every instinct he had developed over the years at sea.

Then, suddenly, a faint glimmer caught his eye. It was just a flicker, barely perceptible against the dark expanse of the water, but it was there. He squinted, trying to focus on the source of the light, his heart pounding with a mix of hope and anxiety.

"Look there," he said, pointing towards the faint light in the distance. The crew's attention snapped to the direction of his gesture, their eyes straining to see what he had seen. The searchlights swung around, their beams converging on the spot their captain had indicated.

In that moment, as the light cut through the darkness, hope flickered to life on the bridge of the MV *Kurasova*. They were not alone in this vast, unforgiving ocean. Someone was out there, waiting to be rescued.

Chapter 18

A Ray of Hope

⋯✦⋯

As the minutes ticked on, the passage of time was marked by the anxious thrum of the hearts of the three souls in the life raft. Each beat seemed to echo with their mounting tension and the desperate hope for rescue. The sea beneath them seemed to grow wilder, each wave a reminder of how fragile their raft was. Then, as if by some miracle, Willy's voice rang out, sharp and urgent, cutting through the despair.

"There! There… there!" he shouted, his eyes wide, staring into the distance.

Christy and Juan followed his gaze, their hearts leaping to their throats. At first, it was just a faint glimmer on the horizon, almost indistinguishable from the countless tricks of light that the ocean played on weary eyes. But this was different. It was stronger, brighter—a beam of hope slicing through the dark, the unmistakable searchlight of a ship.

They weren't hallucinating. The light grew brighter, more focused, and then, cutting through the roar of the sea, they heard it—the deep, resonant blast of a ship's horn. It was a sound that tore through the air, carrying with it the promise of salvation. It was the sound of life.

Juan, unable to contain his excitement, tried to stand, forgetting the pain in his leg. He fell back instantly, clutching his injured limb, but the elation in his voice was undeniable.

"There's a ship!" he shouted, his voice cracking with emotion. "They're looking for us!"

His mind raced. For the first time since the explosion, the fear that had gripped their hearts began to loosen its hold. The light was real. The sound was real. There was no reason for a ship to be out here, in the middle of the ocean, using its searchlight and horn unless they were searching for someone. They weren't going to die out here, not tonight. But they had to act quickly. If they wanted to be rescued, they had to make their presence known, to signal the ship before it was too late.

Juan's hands moved quickly, despite the pain that shot through his body with every motion. He reached for the distress signal, a rocket parachute flare, his fingers trembling as he loaded it. He aimed toward the sky, holding his breath, and fired. The flare shot upwards, a streak of fire piercing the darkness, climbing higher and higher until it reached its apex. There, it exploded in a brilliant burst of orange, lighting up the night like the sun. The flare's bright parachute floated down slowly, casting an eerie glow over the scene, its light reflecting off the water and illuminating the life raft below.

For a moment, time seemed to stand still. The three men stared at the glowing orange parachute, hope and fear battling for dominance in their hearts. Then, through the fading light, they saw it, emerging from the shadows like a giant from the depths. A massive container ship, its towering hull and superstructure unmistakable against the backdrop of the night. It was real. Their salvation had arrived.

Chapter 19

You Are Not Alone

—◆—

MV KURASOVA
PACIFIC OCEAN

An orange light illuminated the entire area, casting an eerie glow over the scene. Everyone's eyes turned skyward, watching a tiny bright orange parachute descend slowly through the air. It was a signal, a beacon of hope in the darkness.

"Gentlemen, we have someone around!" Bijoy screamed, adrenaline surging through his veins.

"Raja, come to the heading 225 degrees. Engine half ahead," he commanded, altering the vessel's course to the distress position and increasing speed slightly.

"Point the searchlights to thirty degrees starboard. All eyes to the starboard side," he instructed. This signal would help the potential survivors know that rescue was on the way.

"There! There, thirty degrees on the starboard side!" Andrei shouted, pointing at the radar screen. A yellow dot appeared, faint but unmistakable.

Captain Bijoy, peering through his night vision binoculars, felt a spine-chilling sensation travel to his brain. There, in the water, was a life raft, a small, fragile orange dot in the vast sea.

"Engine dead slow ahead," he ordered, reducing the ship's speed as they approached the life raft. He adjusted the heading to keep the object ten degrees to starboard.

"All eyes ten degrees to starboard!" he commanded over the public address system.

Captain Bijoy knew this operation would be anything but easy. Maneuvering a mammoth 366-meter-long ship close to a 2-meter-long inflatable raft was a daunting task. He prayed silently for the strength and precision needed to save these lives. Typically, ships approaching port had the assistance of tugs to control their movements; here, they had no such luxury. Yet, in this challenging moment, he recognized a profound blessing—the chance to save lives at sea, the dream of every sailor.

As the ship inched closer, Captain Bijoy assessed the weather conditions. The wind and waves came from the northern direction, so they needed to position north of the life raft to provide shelter. The ship would act as a barrier, reducing wind and waves for the life raft. He outlined the plan clearly.

"Bridge, we can see three people in the life raft," a sailor on the main deck reported over the VHF radio.

All crew members focused their attention on the life raft, the searchlight beam illuminating it starkly against the dark sea. Despite the rain and cold, they saw the desperate faces of the people in the raft, their eyes filled with both hope and fear.

"Bosun, prepare the heaving line on the starboard side," Bijoy ordered.

"Copied, Sir."

"Lower the pilot ladder on the starboard side," he added. "Chief, we will keep the life raft on our starboard side. As we get closer, we will throw the heaving line to the life raft. Once they catch and connect the line, we will pull them in closer, and they can board the ship via the pilot ladder."

Easier said than done, Bijoy thought to himself, but there was no room for doubt.

Gregory and Lewis prepared the pilot ladder meticulously. The vessel moved slowly, the life raft becoming clearer with each passing moment. They heard the cries from the raft, saw the waving arms and folded hands, the survivors' desperate plea for rescue.

"Survivors? Not yet," Bijoy reminded himself. "Not until they're safe aboard this ship."

Twenty-five crew members aboard the 366-meter-long ship, and three souls adrift in a tiny life raft. The magnitude of the task before them was immense, but they were ready. Every sailor knew that tonight, they were not just crew members; they were lifesavers, answering the call of the sea with unwavering determination.

Chapter 20

A Mission to Remember

PACIFIC OCEAN

The vessel crept towards the life raft with a measured, almost delicate precision, the bow thruster's hum filling the cold, tense air. The people in the raft, battered by the elements and teetering on the edge of despair, felt dwarfed by the immense silhouette of the ship. It loomed like a towering cliff.

"Command Station, I can see them clearly now," Gregory reported, his voice crackling with urgency. "Two people standing and one lying down. One chamber of the life raft is punctured."

"Roger, Chief. Do you think they can climb the pilot ladder?" Captain Bijoy's voice, calm but with an undercurrent of concern, came over the radio.

"Negative, all three look terribly tired, and the one lying down appears to be in severe pain. I think we'll have to use the lifeboat," Gregory reported.

"Definitely, we have to do that," Bijoy replied. "In the meantime, throw the heaving line and make contact with the raft," the captain said into the VHF receiver.

Lewis moved with calm precision despite the mounting tension. His weathered hands, steady and sure, deftly coiled a small length of rope - the weighted monkey fist. With a powerful swing, he launched the rope into the air, his movements fluid and confident. The rope arced gracefully, cutting through the misty air before landing with pinpoint accuracy on the life raft.

Christy, exhausted and barely holding on, saw the lifeline land within reach. Summoning the last reserves of his strength, he extended a trembling hand and clutched the line. His grip was weak, but he held on, driven by a fierce will to survive.

"Connect that end to your life raft," Gregory shouted through the loud hailer, his voice cutting through the howling wind.

Christy and Willy, guided by Juan, tied the line securely. "Connected, connected," they shouted, their voices carrying a mix of relief and urgency.

Lewis attached a heavier rope to the other end of the heaving line.

"Pull the line towards you," Gregory instructed.

The two old friends, their fingers numb but their will unbroken, pulled the rope towards them. When the heavier rope reached the raft, they secured it tightly. The life raft was now tethered to the ship, bobbing in the turbulent waters just six meters away—close, yet not close enough.

"Rescue team, proceed to the lifeboat," Captain Bijoy ordered, his tone brooking no hesitation. He knew the gravity of the situation: three lives depended on the swift, precise actions of his men, who would have to leave the safety of the ship and proceed to the life raft.

The rescue team, comprising Chief Officer Gregory, Third Engineer Rohit, and sailors Ivan and Ricardo, sprinted to the lifeboat deck. Donning their life jackets, they prepared for the task ahead. Gregory, the commander of the seven-meter-long orange rescue boat, checked it with a swift eye.

"Captain, lifeboat checked and found in order. Requesting permission to enter," Gregory reported, his voice steady.

"Permission granted," Bijoy replied, his calm demeanor masking the tension he felt.

The four-man squad climbed onto the lifeboat, securing themselves with seat belts. The boat itself, held by wire ropes, was suspended twenty meters above the water.

"Rescue boat team, are you ready?" Bijoy's voice came through the radio, the calm in his tone a steadying force.

"Yes, Captain, we are ready."

"Are you all secure?"

"Yes, Captain."

"Gentlemen, lower the lifeboat and don't stop until you hit the water," he commanded, taking a deep, steadying breath.

Gregory, gripping the wire handle inside the lifeboat, exchanged a resolute glance with his team. He could feel their trust and the weight of the expectations of the lives they were about to save. With a decisive pull, he released the brake. The wire rope uncoiled with a metallic screech, and the boat descended rapidly.

In the life raft, the three men watched intently as the lifeboat descended, its orange form rushing towards the churning sea. Within seconds, the boat splashed down, sending a spray of water in all directions.

"Remove the boat hooks," Bijoy commanded, seeing the lifeboat stable in the water but still attached to the wire ropes.

Gregory activated the hook release lever, and the boat detached from the wire rope and the ship, now free to maneuver. "Hook released. We are proceeding to the life raft," Gregory reported.

"Roger, Chief. Proceed," came the steady response from Captain Bijoy.

Gregory engaged the lifeboat's engine and it moved forward, cutting through the waves. The boat pushed through the water, drawing ever closer to the life raft. For the survivors, every meter closed felt like a lifetime. Juan, seeing the lifeboat approach, felt the tears well up in his eyes. The lifeboat looked like an angel, an orange savior sent by his daughter's daily prayers.

Chapter 21

Return to Life

PACIFIC OCEAN

After four minutes of precise maneuvering in the turbulent Pacific Ocean, the orange lifeboat approached the life raft, guided by the strong search light from the ship. The towering silhouette of the *MV Kurasova* stood sentinel on one side, its immense structure a protective barrier, like a mother shielding her child from the vastness of the ocean.

"Ivan, Ricardo—get the boat hook and secure that life raft!" Gregory's voice sliced through the tension, crisp and authoritative.

There was no room for error now. The two men sprang into action, wrenching open the lifeboat door. They extended the boat hook, stretching towards the life raft that was barely clinging to the surface of the sea. Although the ocean was relatively calm, a light drizzle and the rhythmic rise and fall of small waves conspired to make the task treacherous.

Finally, after what felt like an interminable wait, the hook caught the raft. The men pulled it closer, their muscles straining under the effort. They quickly lashed a thin rope between the lifeboat and the raft, creating a tenuous lifeline. However, as the raft drifted alongside them, it was clear that it was in dire straits—one chamber was deflated, a gaping wound in its side.

Gregory, the rescue commander who had been quietly observing, felt a swell of admiration for the three souls huddled within the raft. Their faces were gaunt, their eyes hollow with exhaustion, yet they had held on. They had fought the sea and lived to see another day. Without a word, he vacated the seat and moved toward the lifeboat door.

"Rohit, secure yourself and help the survivors aboard," he ordered. "Be prepared – they'll be exhausted and likely suffering from hypothermia."

"Ivan, get the thermal protective clothing ready. As soon as they're on-board, we need to act quickly," he continued.

Rohit nodded curtly, securing himself to the lifeboat's railing. He positioned himself cautiously, one foot in the lifeboat, the other on the slippery surface of the raft. The cold spray of seawater and the slick surface beneath him made balancing a near-impossible feat, even for a man of his athletic prowess. He stretched out his hand. "Come on, grab my hand!" he shouted, his voice cutting through the wind.

Willy reached out a trembling hand, gripping Rohit's firmly. He was pulled into the lifeboat, collapsing onto the floor, every ounce of strength drained from his body. "Please help him. His leg's broken," Christy pleaded, pointing to Juan, who was still slumped in the raft.

Rohit looked over at Juan, who was grimacing in pain. "Let's get you in first," Rohit insisted, carefully helping Christy climb into the lifeboat. "Then I'll go for him."

Christy hesitated but obeyed, his movements sluggish as he climbed into the relative safety of the lifeboat.

"Juan can't walk," he repeated, his voice laced with fear and urgency.

Rohit knew what he had to do. Without a second thought, he untied the line securing him to the lifeboat and stepped fully onto the unstable raft. It was a blatant breach of protocol, but protocol be damned—there was a life to save. He knelt beside Juan, trying to lift him. "Leave me," Juan muttered, his voice choked with emotion. "I couldn't save my boat. I could not fulfill my duty. I am not fit to be called a seaman. Let me go down with the yacht."

The words were a dagger to Rohit's heart, but he didn't let them take root. There was no time for this. "Not now," he growled, more to himself than to Juan. With a grunt of effort, he hoisted Juan over his shoulder, struggling to maintain his balance on the pitching raft.

Ricardo leaned out from the lifeboat, ready to pull Juan aboard. But in the frantic scramble, Juan slipped from Rohit's grip, his body lurching towards the dark, freezing water. A collective gasp echoed from the ship and the lifeboat alike as they watched in horror. Rohit did not hesitate. He dove after Juan, plunging into the icy water without a second thought. It was another breach of protocol, but in that moment, protocols were nothing more than words on a page.

The cold water closed around Rohit, but he fought his way to the surface, his hand finding purchase in Juan's hair. Gregory, ever vigilant, had already thrown a buoyant line into the water. Rohit snatched it with his free hand, wrapping the line around his wrist as he struggled to keep Juan's head above water. Slowly, painfully, they were pulled back towards the lifeboat, the weight of the sea fighting them every inch of the way.

At last, they reached the side of the lifeboat. Rohit was the last to be hauled aboard, his chest heaving as he sucked in air, his limbs heavy with exhaustion.

From the bridge wing, Bijoy watched the scene unfold with the steady calm of a man who had seen everything the sea had to offer. His face was impassive, but his eyes were sharp, taking in every detail.

"Three survivors and all four rescue team members, safe," Gregory reported, his voice clipped as he shut the lifeboat door.

"Roger that," Bijoy responded. "Return to the ship."

The *MV Kurasova's* crew let out a loud cheer, a cheer tinged with the weight of what they had just witnessed. They knew that the rescue team in the lifeboat was still in the jaws of danger.

The lifeboat began its cautious journey back to the ship, the thin line connecting the lifeboat to the life raft stretched to its limit, quivering under the strain.

Ivan took a moment to sever the connection from the lifeboat.

As the lifeboat neared the ship, Gregory's voice rang out once more, "Ivan, Ricardo, get the hooks ready!" Despite their exhaustion, the two men snapped into action. They removed their seatbelts and readied the boat hooks, eyes locked on the hanging wire hooks swaying in the night air.

They caught the hooks on the first attempt, securing the lifeboat in place. Gregory activated the locking mechanism, ensuring the hooks were firmly in place and the lifeboat was safely locked before giving the order to secure the seatbelts.

Rohit and Ivan moved quickly, strapping in the survivors, while Ricardo shut the lifeboat door with a finality that echoed through the enclosed space. Gregory, now back in control, reported over the VHF, "We're all secured."

"Well done, Chief. We are heaving you up now. See you on deck," came the captain's steady reply.

"Bosun, heave the lifeboat," Bijoy ordered, his voice carrying over the radio. Lewis, his hands steady on the lifeboat winch remote, pressed the button. The winch groaned to life, the wire rope straining as it began to lift the lifeboat out of the water.

"Second Officer, cut the line to the life raft," Bijoy commanded. Moving with great care, Amol severed the last connection between the ship and the tiny life raft, which had, until recently, held three human lives in its precarious bosom. He watched as the raft, now adrift, began its slow descent into the abyss, its purpose fulfilled.

Inside the lifeboat, Christy, Willy, and Juan heard the command over the VHF. They knew that the raft that had borne them for the last three harrowing hours was about to disappear beneath the waves. There was a moment of silence, a shared understanding of the gravity of the moment. They longed to look back; to take one final glance at the fragile vessel that had kept them alive, but Gregory, ever the disciplinarian, forbade it. The seatbelts remained fastened, the raft slipped into the depths, and the crew on the *MV Kurasova* watched as it vanished and paid a silent tribute to the ocean's power.

The lifeboat's ascent continued, each turn of the winch feeling like an eternity. A heavy silence settled over the crew as they waited. Each inch gained felt like a mile, each creak of the wire rope a grim reminder of the perilous nature of their situation.

Finally, after what felt like an endless struggle, the lifeboat reached the cradle of its mother ship, the *MV Kurasova*. The relief was almost overwhelming as the boat settled into place. Bosun Lewis and the other sailors moved quickly, securing the boat with additional lashings, making sure it was firmly in place before opening the door.

Rohit was the first to step out, his body aching, his clothes soaked through, but his mind clear. He held the door open as Christy and Willy followed, their faces streaked with tears. They stumbled from the lifeboat, their bodies wrapped in blankets by the waiting crew, their tears falling unchecked as the reality of their rescue began to sink in.

A stretcher was brought into the lifeboat for Juan. Under Gregory's careful instructions, Ivan and Ricardo lifted him onto the stretcher, strapping him in with gentle hands. Despite his injury, Juan's eyes were filled with a quiet pride – a will to survive that had been tested by the ocean but not broken. The crew saluted him as he was carried from the lifeboat, acknowledging his bravery and the ordeal he had survived.

Chief Officer Gregory was the last to step out of the lifeboat. He paused, glancing back at the lifeboat, then bent down to kiss its side – a gesture of gratitude and respect. Straightening up, he looked toward the bridge wing, locking eyes with the captain. With a slight, almost imperceptible nod, he raised his hand to his temple in a crisp salute. No words were exchanged, but the gesture spoke volumes – a silent acknowledgment of a mission well-executed, a shared understanding between two seasoned sailors. The captain returned the salute with a faint smile, his eyes reflecting a mixture of pride and relief. The operation was over, and they had emerged victorious.

The silence that had held the ship in its grip broke at last. A wave of celebration rippled through the crew, laughter and shouts of relief filling the night air. They had saved three lives from the clutches of the deep, and now it was time to rejoice.

As the survivors were taken to the ship's hospital, the crew embraced each other, tears and smiles mingling as they celebrated their successful mission.

Chapter 22

Breath of Relief

—◆—

MV KURASOVA
PACIFIC OCEAN
MRCC GERMANY
AUCKLAND

Bijoy reached into his pocket and pulled out a slightly crumpled pack of Marlboro Red. With a flick of his wrist, he tapped out a cigarette, then, with ease, flipped open his Zippo lighter. His thumb struck the flint wheel, igniting the flame. In one smooth motion, he brought it to the cigarette, lighting it before snapping the lighter shut with a satisfying click. He took a deep drag, letting the nicotine fill his lungs, savoring the taste before exhaling a thick cloud of white smoke into the air.

"Third, dial the number to the rescue center," he instructed Andrei, his voice steady but filled with the weight of the last few hours.

Andrei dialed the satellite phone, connecting to the MRCC in Germany. The call was answered before the first ring had even fully echoed through the bridge.

"Rescue Coordination Centre, Germany," came the brisk, professional greeting on the other end.

"This is the Captain of the *MV Kurasova*."

"Yes, Captain, please go ahead," Bernard, the station commander, replied, his voice tinged with excitement and uncertainty, unsure whether the captain's news would be good or bad.

"Please note this down: at local time 0430 hours, we rescued three men from the ocean and brought them aboard," Captain Bijoy reported, his voice betraying none of the tension that had gripped the ship during the operation.

There was a pause on the other end, and then an exclamation, "Oh my holy God! That's fantastic!" The commander's voice rang out, filling the room where he sat. He shot out of his chair; his thumb thrust high into the air as he signaled the news to his team, the tension of the hours-long vigil breaking like a dam.

"We will be sending a detailed event report soon," Bijoy continued, his tone still measured.

"Thank you so much, Captain. Please take your time," the commander replied, his voice barely concealing the excitement. The call ended, but the jubilation had just begun.

The room erupted in cheers. Emma, who had been pacing anxiously, grabbed Alder in a tight hug, both of them jumping up and down like schoolchildren who had just been given a holiday.

"One minute," Emma said, her voice catching in her throat. "Shall we inform Robert?"

The commander nodded, his expression softening as he reached for the phone again. This call required a gentler touch. He dialed the number, and within seconds, the phone was answered.

"Hello, Robert here," came the voice, strained with the weight of the hours spent in agonized waiting and wondering.

"Robert, happy news!" the commander burst out, unable to contain his joy. "Your father and the other two survivors were rescued by a merchant ship just about ten minutes ago." Then, in a gentler tone, he said, "They're safe. You'll see them soon."

There was a pause, a breath caught in the chest, and then Robert's voice broke through, choked with emotion. "Thank you… thank you so much," he said, his grip tightening around the receiver.

"Thanks are not for us, Robert," the commander said gently. "They're for the sailors on that ship. Now, go get some sleep." He knew, of course, that sleep would be the farthest thing from Robert's mind tonight. However, the message had been delivered, and the call was ended.

Robert, still clutching the phone, looked down at the family photo on the table beside him, his father smiling; that smile will not have its sun set soon. He kissed it, his tears soaking into the frame as he whispered a silent prayer of thanks.

He returned to the bedroom where Sofia and their daughter lay sleeping, unaware of the drama that had just unfolded. He touched Sofia's cheek, a soft, lingering caress, and kissed her gently, careful not to wake her. Then, with a heart finally lightened by relief, he lay down beside her.

Chapter 23

The MV Kurasova and Her Crew

The survivors huddled together in the hospital, their faces pale and drawn, still grappling with the trauma of the last few hours. Christy and Willy clung to each other, their hands trembling, yet a glimmer of gratitude shone in their eyes as they whispered words of thanks to the ship's crew. They knew they had nothing left—no clothes, no documents, no money—nothing. Yet, they were deeply thankful for the crew's help, despite knowing nothing about them.

Gregory knelt beside them, his voice steady and reassuring, as he placed a warm blanket over their shoulders. Amol, with a practiced calm, examined Juan's leg, his hands moving deftly as he splinted the fracture, wrapping it with great care.

In the galley, the chief cook stirred a pot of soup, its rich aroma wafting through the narrow corridors. He ladled out steaming bowlfuls and delivered them to the survivors personally, his rough hands surprisingly gentle as he placed the bowls into their trembling hands—a much-needed gesture to help them fend off the cold.

Up on the bridge, Bijoy stood, a solitary figure silhouetted against the vast expanse of the ocean. The light from his cigarette flickered briefly before he extinguished it, the faint smell of tobacco lingering in the air. He picked up the phone and dialed the engine room, his voice carrying the weight of responsibility as he spoke into the receiver.

"Chief, the mission was successful. We're resuming our passage."

From the other end, Rajesh's voice crackled to life, a note of excitement clear even through the static.

"We're ready, Captain. The engine's at your disposal."

"When are you starting on that mountainous paperwork?" he asked after a pause, his voice teasing as he indirectly referred to the reports that needed to be filed with various authorities about the rescue operation.

Bijoy allowed himself a laugh. "Don't worry. I'll start the reports after a couple of Vodka Martinis."

"Shaken, not stirred," Rajesh replied with a chuckle, the camaraderie of fifteen years evident in his tone.

"Precisely," Bijoy murmured, "Shaken, not stirred. The double-oh seven way." his voice tinged with a rare moment of levity.

As he ended the call, Captain Bijoy's face grew serious once more. He pressed the intercom button and spoke into the public address system, his voice steady and authoritative.

"Gentlemen," He took a pause, allowing everyone to listen, and then he continued,

"Gentlemen, Brave hearts, we are resuming the voyage. Secure everything on deck and prepare to continue. Thank you for your exceptional work."

His words echoed throughout the ship, a call to action that was met with a flurry of movement as the crew sprang to life.

Bijoy turned back to the window, his gaze distant, as he watched the horizon. A single tear slid down his weathered cheek, though his expression remained stoic, a faint smile tugging at the corners of his lips. The darkness of the bridge concealed his emotions from the crew, but inside, he felt pride.

"Dead slow ahead," he commanded, his voice firm as he pointed his fingers forward in the direction of the next port.

Third Officer Andrei moved the telegraph, the metallic clink resonating through the bridge as the engine responded, the deep hum of the machinery reverberating through the hull. The ship lurched forward, the propeller churning the water, leaving a frothy wake in its path. The vessel, their stalwart lady, surged ahead, cutting through the waves.

The captain stood silently, his hand resting on the railing as he felt the familiar vibrations beneath his feet. They had ports to reach, oceans to cross, and as long as there was water under the keel, they would keep moving forward.

This was the life of a sailor, bound to the sea, devoted to the ship, and ever ready to face whatever lay beyond the horizon.

Epilogue I

Two Years After the Successful Rescue Operation in the Pacific Ocean

As the setting sun painted the Auckland sky with its final, fiery hues, it created a masterpiece that stretched across the horizon. Below this celestial canvas, the grand, white mansion stood majestically, bathed in twilight's soft embrace. The lush, vibrant lawn mirrored its elegance. String lights twinkled softly, casting a gentle, enchanting glow over the evening, creating an atmosphere of serene beauty.

Tables were meticulously set with crisp white linens, adorned with vases brimming with fresh roses and peonies. Comfortable lounge areas, featuring plush cushions in soft blush and ivory, enticed guests to unwind and savor the evening's offerings. A large sign at the entrance of the lawn proudly announced: **"WELCOME, OUR HEROES."**

Robert and Sofia were busy with last-minute checks, ensuring every detail was perfect for the evening. Anna and Maria were putting the final touches on the buffet area, while Annette and Adriana playfully shared a teddy bear, adding a touch of innocent joy to the scene.

Christy, Willy and Juan stood eagerly at the entrance, their faces alight with anticipation and gratitude. They were thrilled to host this special evening for the brave hearts who had once saved their lives at sea— the crew members of *MV Kurasova*.

As guests arrived, they were greeted with flutes of the finest champagne, its effervescence catching the last light of day, adding a sparkle to the occasion. The champagne was paired with smoked salmon, truffle-infused mushroom tartlets, and delicate crab cakes. For those seeking alternatives, a well-stocked bar offered a selection of fine wines, craft cocktails, and refreshing non-alcoholic options.

At one end of the garden, an intimate stage had been set up, draped with flowing fabrics. Soft, warm lights illuminated the stage, creating a perfect backdrop for the evening's entertainment. The air was filled with the smooth melodies of a live jazz band.

The crew members and their families gathered under the twinkling lights, their faces lit by the soft, golden glow of patio lights swaying gently in the evening breeze.

Lewis was the first to arrive at the function, getting to the venue before anyone else. He assisted the hosts with the preparations, displaying his expertise. Captain Bijoy arrived with his wife, Priya, and their precious baby girl, Amiya. Rajesh Kumar strolled in alongside his Portuguese wife.

Amol, the confirmed bachelor, had arrived two days earlier. He was already in high spirits, often found teasing Rohit and his wife, Paro, with his characteristic sense of humor. Gregory and Nikolay Plaman arrived solo, each bringing their own unique charm to the gathering. Raja made his entrance with his wife, both beaming with the contentment of the moment.

Ernesto and Rizilino, seamen from the Philippines, were taken aback by the invitation and the impressive arrangements that greeted them. As the youngest crew members of the *MV Kurasova*, they hadn't expected to attend such an extravagant party.

Andrei and his girlfriend had arrived just a couple of hours earlier, their energy and enthusiasm a lively addition to the party. The air was electric with happiness as everyone exchanged hearty greetings and warm embraces, the sense of camaraderie and joy palpable throughout the evening.

It had taken meticulous planning to bring this event to life. Christy and Willy, the masterminds behind the gathering, had known it would be impossible to gather the entire crew, with many still at sea. To get around this, they set a date six months in advance, allowing crew members to adjust their schedules and secure time off. They had also reached out to members of the Maritime Rescue Control Center in Germany, but strict protocols made their participation impossible. Ultimately, twelve crew members, a few with family, were able to attend.

By seven in the evening, the party was in full swing. The lawn buzzed with the energy of the reunion, filled with laughter and animated conversations that spoke of shared experiences and deep bonds.

Juan, who had spent months recovering from his injury, now moved through the crowd with an easy grace. His wife and daughter, now settled in New Zealand, radiated contentment, their smiles reflecting the joy of their new life.

Robert, Sofia and Anna moved among their guests with effortless grace, their faces radiant with the deep satisfaction of hosting those who had played a crucial role in saving their loved ones.

As the evening deepened, the conversations grew livelier. Each guest had a story to tell, and the air was thick with nostalgia, a shared pride binding everyone together. At a quarter to nine, Christy took to the microphone, his voice cutting through the hum of conversation with clear, resonant warmth.

"Ladies and Gentlemen," he began, his tone both welcoming and theatrical, "how is the evening?"

The response was a chorus of cheers and applause, a testament to the high spirits of the gathering.

"We are here because of the bravery and dedication of the gentlemen of *MV Kurasova*," Christy continued, his gaze sweeping through the crowd. "Let's raise our glasses to that unforgettable night."

Glasses clinked in a harmonious toast, the sound echoing like a jubilant symphony under the night sky. As the applause subsided, Christy paused, his expression turning thoughtful.

"I still remember that night on the *Odyssey* with striking clarity. It began like any other day, cruising smoothly, until suddenly, in the dead of night, the fuel oil filter cover in the engine room gave way while I was on night watch. In an instant, oil began spraying onto the hot surfaces nearby, landing with a sizzling hiss." He paused and took a walk on the stage, "Juan had performed a temporary repair a couple of days earlier, but clearly, it wasn't enough. The fire spread everywhere, engulfing our small yacht."

"It was devastating to watch it become consumed by flames, and finally, it ended with a massive explosion, turning the yacht into a fiery ball of destruction."

"Amid the chaos," he continued, "Juan's courage and quick thinking were our saving grace. Moreover, I like to think it wasn't just luck that got us out of that mess; it felt as though divine intervention played a role."

"What if our EPIRB signal had been lost in the sky? What if the signal hadn't been picked up by the satellite and relayed to the correct rescue center? What if the *MV Kurasova* hadn't been nearby? What if Amol, the second officer, had ignored the distress message?" Christy pondered aloud, his gaze thoughtful.

"The truth is, what I want to believe is that someone wanted us to live a little longer, to be here today for this gathering," he said with a warm smile.

Willy took over the microphone, "We know each other well by now," he said softly. "But through our journey from the Yelapa Boat Club in Mexico to New Zealand, one thing became clear: the sea has many faces, many myths, and countless stories to tell."

The sea, with its mysteries and dangers, had been the force that brought them together. They were not just celebrating a heroic rescue tonight but also the enduring spirit of those who dared to brave the unknown.

"These gentlemen," Willy said, his voice filled with reverence, "these seamen, are the true bearers of the sea's legacy. They work far from home, moving cargo that keeps the world turning."

He paused again, letting the weight of his words sink in. "Now, let us hear from them—the stories of the sea."

As the evening began to unfold, it set the stage for the masters of the seas to take the crowd on an unforgettable journey.

"Do we have a volunteer to start with?" Willy asked, scanning the crowd with a warm smile.

"I think we should not disturb the Captain and the Chief Engineer this evening. Let them sit back and relax while others talk," Christy chimed in, his eyes twinkling with mischief.

Christy and Willy left the stage and approached their guests, slowly moving towards the bosun.

"Let's invite Mr Lewis to the stage," Christy announced. "He's likely spent more time at sea than anyone else here."

"Let's give a big round of applause to the tycoon of the seas, the esteemed keeper of the ships, the bosun himself!"

LEWIS – Served as bosun on the *MV Kurasova*

Lewis was taken aback by the unexpected call to the stage but was clearly touched. Setting his whisky down, he made his way to the stage amidst the enthusiastic applause of the crowd.

As he took the microphone, he paused and looked out at the audience.

"Can I speak without the mic? This thing is really uncomfortable," Lewis asked with a chuckle.

"No problem, Lewis. The stage is yours. You're the Boss," Willy replied, nodding encouragingly.

Lewis walked to the front of the stage. As he reached the center, he folded his arms behind his back, "Rotterdam," he began, his voice tinged with a mix of reverence and pain. "It was a night I'll never forget—one of those nights when the sea decides to demonstrate her powers."

He paused for a moment and lifted his shirt to show the stitches from old wounds on his left ribs.

"A gift—from thirty years ago."

A few gasps came from the audience.

"I was just twenty-one then, fresh out at sea and brimming with dreams as I boarded my first ship. Back then, the vessels were old and the rules were much more lenient than they are today. There was rust everywhere, and as a trainee seaman under the bosun, I worked tirelessly, feeling like a mere slave. The bosun, Danijel, was more feared than respected. His treatment of trainees was harsh, and his patience non-existent. In the six months I spent with him, I don't recall a single word of praise or appreciation."

Lewis paused for a moment and gazed at the pine trees in the garden, their branches adorned with glowing lights. However, one light was out, and his eyes instinctively sought out the missing part, driven by a need to fix what was incomplete. *No, not today, I am not on the ship*, he reminded himself.

The memory of Danijel's harshness remained vivid in his mind. "Danijel never missed a chance to drive us hard. We worked from dawn until dusk, and often well beyond. He had a way of breaking you down until all that was left was sheer, relentless perseverance. It was his method, and though we never complained, it often felt more like punishment than training."

He took the microphone from Willy. "That crazy night in Rotterdam," Lewis said, gripping the microphone, "the wind was wild. The mooring ropes were straining, and each gust pushed the ship harder against its lines."

"Half the crew were out on shore leave when the weather took a sudden turn. With the port closed and cargo operations halted, those of us left behind were scrambling to secure the vessel alongside the jetty, working with fourteen heavy ropes in the winches."

"Bosun and I were in the forward mooring station where we had to deal with seven such ropes, pushing ourselves to adjust them. It was cold, with a biting wind that carried a slight drizzle, making the night even more miserable. To my surprise, he asked me to stand in the middle of the ropes under stress and relay information about them while he worked adjacent to the winch, which was a relatively safer place. I faced him, fully aware of the amount of force stored in those massive ropes. My fear grew with each creak, the ominous sound of ropes under stress. Every groan felt like a prelude to disaster."

Lewis' eyes clouded as he remembered the terror of the moment. "The wind picked up ferociously. The ropes were groaning, on the brink of snapping. Danijel, harsh as he was, knew how to handle the ropes, but that night, even his expertise was barely enough to cope with nature's fury. He was pushing me towards death."

Lewis leaned forward, his voice dropping to a whisper. "I was in a dangerous spot, caught between the ropes and the howling wind. Danijel realized what was about to happen. Without a second thought, he jumped at me, shoving me out of the way. I stumbled over a rope and fell hard onto the deck below, breaking several of my ribs. He stood there—a brief moment of defiance—before the inevitable happened. One of the ropes finally gave way."

"The snap was deafening. The severed rope lashed out like a serpent, striking Danijel with brutal force."

Lewis's face softened with a mixture of sorrow and respect. "In that instant, Danijel's harshness seemed to vanish. He was no longer just a taskmaster but a man who chose to save me, even at the cost of his own life. The rope struck him with a ferocity that no man could survive. The blood, the chaos—it all happened so quickly."

He looked up, meeting the eyes of his captive audience with solemn intensity. "Danijel's sacrifice wasn't something I understood at the time. He was a harsh man, one who seemed to take pleasure in making our lives difficult. But he was preparing us, preparing us for the harsh reality of life at sea."

The crowd fell silent, the weight of the story hanging heavily in the air.

"That night in Rotterdam remains a testament to the unexpected courage and compassion that can emerge from even the most hardened of hearts."

As Lewis finished his tale, the crowd remained silent, unsure whether to clap or not. The atmosphere was thick with the weight of his story. Sensing the tension, Willy stepped onto the stage, lightening the mood.

"That was quite an experience to share, Lewis, and you are truly a hero," he said, his voice warm and encouraging. "You carry the weight of responsibility that Mr Danijel handed over to you."

Christy gestured for Robert to guide Lewis back to his chair.

Willy then turned to the audience with a smile. "Now, let's listen to some music before we move on to the next story. We are in for a treat from our superstars of the *MV Kurasova*, Ernesto and Rizilino. They were seamen working under Bosun Lewis, and I believe this was their first ship."

"That's correct, it was our first ship," Rizilino replied, his excitement evident. Both he and Ernesto were pumped up for the occasion, eager to showcase their talent.

They seized the opportunity, and as they began to sing, the live jazz music added a professional touch to their performance. For the next thirty minutes, they entertained the guests, shifting the mood away from the somber story of Danijel's tragic death and Lewis's injuries. The garden filled with the lively jazz rhythms, and slowly, the mood lightened, replaced by the sheer joy of music.

The appreciative audience erupted in applause and cheers as the duo concluded their final song. The energy in the air was palpable, with waves of excitement rolling through the audience.

Moments later, Willy and Christy reappeared on stage, their presence commanding attention once more. They made their way toward Gregory, the Chief Officer of the *MV Kurasova*—the man who had commanded the lifeboat that saved the survivors in the vast Pacific Ocean.

"Hey, Gregory," Willy began with a smile, "I remember the first thing I saw through the lifeboat window was your eyes. There was a spark, a certain determination." He paused, looking at him with curiosity. "Can you share some stories from your sea life with us? I know you're not as serious as you look."

Gregory, usually the embodiment of discipline and duty, found himself in an unusual state of leisure. The man was liberated from the shackles of his responsibilities. This was a rare moment when the crew would see him without his characteristic serious expression.

As he stepped onto the small stage in the garden, holding a glass of fine vodka, there was almost complete silence. The crew, who had grown accustomed to his stern, efficient demeanor during drills, looked on with a mix of curiosity and anticipation. They knew Gregory's flair for drama, but it was always within the context of duty.

Gregory took a large gulp of vodka, savouring the moment, and he was ready to let the vodka speak for him.

GREGORY – Served as the Chief Officer on the *MV Kurasova*

"Hey everyone, let me take you back to this wild experience we had in Australia a couple of years ago. Buckle up—this one is a rollercoaster!"

The crowd shifted in their seats, their attention sharpening, eager to hear Gregory speak. He looked around, a slight smile breaking his usual grim countenance.

"It was our maiden voyage to Australia, and we all knew how stringent their inspections could be. They have no tolerance for substandard ships entering their waters. So, we pulled out all the stops, working tirelessly day and night to prepare our good old lady for the inspection from the groom's side. We scrubbed every inch of her until she gleamed like a brand-new penny. Honestly, if our ship were a person, she would have been picked by any man on Earth.

The Port State Control inspector came aboard on our arrival and gave us a thumbs-up in record time. We were over the moon, and our captain promised us a party near the Sydney Opera House. We were all picturing ourselves sipping cold beers, gazing at the Sydney Harbour Bridge and dreaming of fireworks."

Gregory continued narrating using his entire body. Suddenly, he paused.

"Then, BAM, plot twist! Over the radio, we hear, 'Two visitors from Biosecurity on-board.' And we're like, 'Biosecurity? Did we just sign up for an extra inspection or something?' But, sure enough, the two biosecurity officers walked into the ship's office dressed like they were auditioning for the next sci-fi blockbuster—masks, gloves, the whole get-up.

They flashed their badges with all the drama of a James Bond movie scene, launching into a lecture about protecting Australia from 'potentially dangerous species.' Apparently, lab-grown organisms could wreak havoc on the local ecosystems around the world, and foreign waters were a ticking time bomb of microorganisms."

Gregory mimicked the biosecurity officer's stern demeanour, straightening his posture and fixing his gaze forward with unblinking intensity. He raised his finger, pointing dramatically as if delivering a crucial warning.

"The world is edging towards a biological war—a conflict not with guns, but with pathogens designed to make us ill, devastate our environment, and turn us into perpetual seekers of medicine. Australia and other nations are bracing themselves for potential bioweapon attacks aimed at destroying our ecosystems and living creatures.

As they spoke with grim determination, all I could think was, 'Seriously? I just want to kick back and watch the fireworks with a cold beer in hand!'

But practically, we were confident about any kind of inspection. We had prepared our good lady so well that she was as clean as a whistle.

The officers sat on the other side of the table with a three-page checklist in their hands.

The steward brought coffee and snacks for the biosecurity officers, but they declined with a look of suspicion, as if fearing that the refreshments might be harbouring a viral threat from the ship.

Then came the grilling.

'Do you have any pets on-board?'

'Nope.'

'Any open food items lying around?'

'Not a crumb.'

'Plants?'

'None.'

The captain was starting to sweat bullets as the officers got down to the nitty-gritty—a full-blown physical inspection. They were like detectives with laser pointers, inspecting every nook and cranny: the provision store, mess room, galley—you name it.

Finally, they reached the deck where cargo operations were in full swing. That's when they struck gold—some food grains had spilled onto the deck. Their eyes lit up like they'd discovered buried treasure. The lady officer, with all the seriousness of a judge presiding over a high-profile case, pointed out a tiny ant among the grains.

'Mr. Chief Officer, what was your last port?'

'Shanghai, China,' I replied.

'Do you see this?' she continued, her eyes glued to the offending ant.

'Yes, I can. It is an ant,' I responded.

She shook her head and said, 'Look, watch it closely. It's a Chinese ant.'

I nearly fell over. How on earth could she identify a Chinese ant just by looking at it?

'Is there a problem with it?' I asked curiously.

'Of course, there is. It can destroy the balance of our ecological system,' she continued.

I tried to reason with them. 'It is impossible for an ant to survive a fourteen-day voyage. That too in continuous rain and stormy weather.'

But she was not ready to accept that logic.

She started pointing out the lines on the ant's butt, saying, 'These lines are characteristic of Chinese ants.'

I squinted at the ant and thought, 'Oh dear, I can barely see the ant, let alone its butt lines!'

She was adamant. She decreed we needed fumigation, which meant a delay, leaving the ship, and potential commercial havoc."

"Oh crap," Christy interjected, clearly feeling the tension of the story.

"Yeah, we'd have to leave the ship until they finished fumigating it – at least 48 hours. But then, the male officer, who actually seemed impressed with how we had maintained the ship, threw us a lifeline.

'What's your next port?' he asked.

'Melbourne,' I replied.

'Alright. So you have one more Australian port,' he said. 'We'll give you a chance. We'll inspect the ship there. In the meantime, we'll take this ant to our lab for further examination.'

"What a relief! We spent the next three days scouring the ship for any further ant invasions. Crew members were on their hands and knees, meticulously inspecting every inch of the ship. We even washed the deck with seawater as if performing some sort of sacred ritual.

Amid all this frenzy, the captain's family was on-board, and his ten-year-old daughter, Diana, joined in the 'ant hunt' with enthusiasm. She had one condition, though. For every ant that she caught, her father would have to pay her ten dollars.

When we finally docked in Melbourne, no one came to inspect us. Either they decided the ants were Australian now, or they'd figured the ants were just showing off some fancy butt tattoos and weren't a threat after all.

Three tense and hectic days ended with no action, and we shifted the party from Sydney to Melbourne."

"So, in the end, you saved Australia from an epic invasion of Chinese golden ants with stylish tattoos on their butts?" Sofia asked, raising a toast to the sky in appreciation of Gregory's storytelling skills.

"And the best part? No diplomatic incident required!" Gregory stopped and finished his vodka with style.

Soft jazz continued to play behind them as Gregory finished his tale and Christy moved onto the stage.

"That was a truly wonderful story, Chief. We really enjoyed it," he said with a smile, his eyes glinting with amusement.

"I know it's quite funny to talk about it now, but back then, you all must have been really on edge," he observed.

The guests nodded in agreement.

Christy winked at the crowd. "So, who's next?" he pondered, scanning the audience thoughtfully. "Alright, let us call Mr. Raja to the stage."

RAJAPAKSE – Served as a seaman on the *MV Kurasova*

Rajapakse Damitha Bimsara, the Sri Lankan sailor known to everyone as Raja, was seated with his wife and the chief cook in one corner of the lawn, sipping his drink peacefully. His expression said it all – a look of sheer shock upon hearing his name called. He wondered what he could share on stage, feeling a surge of nervousness. Fortunately, Christy, the ever-comforting host, offered him a reassuring smile.

Raja slowly raised himself to his feet, his eyes darting nervously around the gathering. His shirt, well-ironed and neatly tucked in, contrasted sharply with the casual attire of the others. He was dapper even in moments of discomfort.

Christy's voice was soft and soothing. "So, Raja, how are you enjoying the evening?"

Raja cleared his throat. "All good, Sir."

Christy smiled, shaking his head gently. "No need to call me 'Sir,' Raja. Do you remember how well you steered the ship to rescue us?"

"Yes," Raja replied, a faint smile playing on his lips as he recalled the experience. "I remember that day."

"Do you have any stories to share with us?" Christy asked, his eyes twinkling with curiosity.

Raja hesitated, his mind racing through the years he had spent at sea. After a long pause, he began, his voice carrying the unmistakable rhythm of his Sri Lankan accent.

"December 31st, twelve years ago, in the chilly evening of Barcelona. Our ship had been in port for three days, handling cargo operations before heading to New York. It was New Year's Eve, but while most people were preparing for the celebrations, we seamen were busy with our duties."

Gregory, from the audience, voiced his concern, "Oh, crap! Crossing the mighty Atlantic in winter would be rough."

Raja paused and then continued, "After the stevedores had left, we made sure all the containers were securely fastened for the voyage. Next on our agenda was a thorough search for stowaways and contraband."

"Stowaways? You mean illegal emigrants?" Anna asked.

"Yes, exactly," Raja replied, pausing thoughtfully. "The crew was split into teams, each assigned to a different section of the ship for a meticulous sweep. The captain was adamant that we would not overlook even the smallest detail."

"If they didn't check thoroughly, the Americans would have a field day with the ship," Rajesh joked, his mood quite high.

"My team had the cargo loading area to cover," Raja continued. "It was going to be tough—climbing up and down three floors on a vertical ladder, checking between containers. Lots of physical activity.

After about twenty minutes, while my co-searcher and I were still navigating the lashing bridges, the other teams began reporting in.

'Engine room checked, no drugs or stowaways found.'

'Roger that, thank you.'

'Accommodation space checked, no drugs or stowaways found.'

I pushed myself harder, racing through the lashing bridges almost three floors high. Suddenly, I noticed some movement in the gap between two containers. I pulled back, shining my flashlight into the gap.

A chill ran down my spine as I saw a person huddled there, shivering. A thin, gray-haired European man with deep-set eyes, his arms folded tightly, trying to fit himself inside the tiny gap. Our eyes met, and I saw the fear and desperation in his gaze. He was clearly trying to cross the ocean.

'Is he here, hiding for a better life?' I asked myself.

In that fleeting moment, a flood of memories of my brother surged through me. He had once been a seaman, a man who abandoned his ship in Vancouver years ago while the ship was in port, chasing a dream of a better life that never happened. His departure was more than just a physical abandonment; it felt like a deep betrayal of the ship, his comrades, and our family. My anger at him was fierce and unyielding.

Yet, despite the bitterness, he was still my brother. Driven by a mixture of hope and desperation, we reached out to the Canadian consulate, trying to trace his whereabouts.

Then, after a year or so, the news came—he had been apprehended in a remote corner of Canada, detained as an illegal immigrant, living without any papers. The reality of his situation hit me like a cold wave, a cruel reminder of the path he had chosen and the consequences that it entailed.

Now, here was another man, in freezing cold, pleading for my mercy. If I kept silent, he might make it to New York.

The radio continued to shout out the search results from different parts of the ship.

Mooring stations checked, nothing found.

Lifeboats checked, nothing found.

Feeling my strength waning, I stared at the man's anguish. But, as a seaman, I had a responsibility to the ship.

'Command station, stowaway found near the container,' I reported, my voice steady despite the internal conflict.

There was a moment of silence on the radio.

'Can you repeat the last message?' came the response.

'Sir, stowaway on-board,' I repeated. My eyes remained locked on the man as his hope seemed to dim. Tears rolled down his cheeks.

Additional crew members joined us to ensure the stowaway's response was managed. We helped him out of his confined hiding spot and guided him to the main deck. His jacket was torn, and his fingers were red from the cold

The captain was waiting in the ship's office, seated at the long table. The chief officer was on the left, recording events in the logbook, while the chief engineer puffed on a cigar to his right. Everyone aboard was visibly irritated by the unexpected situation."

'Raja, sit down,' the captain instructed. I took my place as the prime witness. The stowaway sat across from the captain, calm but visibly disappointed. Two crew members flanked him, ready for any unexpected moves.

'Someone get him some water,' the captain ordered.

The bosun brought a glass of water for the stowaway.

'Gentleman, what is your name?' the captain asked, his tone even.

'Skutnik,' the stowaway replied, not looking up.

The captain raised his eyebrows. 'Are you Romanian?'

'Yes,' Skutnik said quietly.

The captain, also Romanian, remained stoic. 'Which part of Romania are you from?'

'Buciumeni,' he answered.

The captain understood the dire situation. Buciumeni was known for its extreme poverty, where basic necessities were often a luxury. Nevertheless, it was his duty to ask.

'Why are you on my ship? When did you board, and where were you planning to go?' the captain asked, his sympathy barely concealed.

Skutnik remained silent.

After a moment of tense silence, the captain stood up and slammed his hand on the table, startling everyone in the room. I jumped from my chair in shock.

'Captain, I want to go to America. I want my family to eat every day. I don't want them to die of hunger,' Skutnik said in a single breath.

'Do you understand that crossing the Atlantic in winter is suicide? You could freeze to death,' the captain said, his voice calm but firm.

'Captain, I will not die. Please help me. I will work here. I will do whatever you ask. Please don't throw me out,' Skutnik pleaded, breaking down in tears.

I found myself questioning my decision. No one leaves their home unless it's out of desperation.

'Captain, my family hates me because I can't provide enough food even after working hard the whole day. We live in a one-room apartment with leaks and no proper lock. My wife has to sell her body to feed our children. I cannot even question her because I am not worth it. If I reach America, I will work hard and make a better life for us,' Skutnik cried.

The captain knew that even if Skutnik reached America, he would likely be caught by the Coast Guard and face imprisonment. People often believe that the other side of the ocean will offer a better life, but reality is often harsher than they imagine.

Just then, the Spanish Coast Guard arrived, completing all the necessary formalities. The captain explained the situation in detail, and the chief officer handed over the written record. The Coast Guard officers were ready to take Skutnik into custody.

'Mr Inspector, could you do me a favor?' the captain asked, stopping the officers.

'Of course, Captain. Tell me,' the senior officer replied.

The captain spoke to them privately, his request seeming earnest. After some discussion, the senior Coast Guard officer nodded in agreement.

The captain returned with a satisfied look on his face, took the phone and dialed the mess room, then spoke to the chief cook.

'Chief Cook, please bring a large sandwich and a big pot of coffee for the stowaway,' he ordered. He wanted to give at least one good meal to his fellow countryman before handing him over to the authorities."

Raja finished his story. The crowd fell silent, emotions running high.

"That's an incredible story, Raja. Thank you for sharing it," Christy said, breaking the silence.

"Ladies and gentlemen, we are truly fortunate. When we walk into a fine restaurant, we don't give a second thought to the prices on the menu as we order our meals. But let's take a moment to remember that there are countless people around us who, no matter how hard they work, are not blessed with the simple luxury of filling their stomachs three times a day. While we dine without worry, they struggle just to survive. This is a privilege, and one we should never take for granted." Christy continued as he walked with Raja back to his chair.

After Raja wrapped up his story, Christy eagerly scanned the crowd until he found one of his favorites from the *MV Kurasova*—Andrei. Andrei and his girlfriend were in a cozy corner of the garden at the party, eating delicious steak. Their arrival had been a feat in itself; they had endured a grueling journey from Bulgaria to Dubai, then to Singapore, and finally to Auckland.

Upon reaching Auckland, they discovered that their luggage had been lost in transit. Faced with the tedious process of filing claims and dealing with airport formalities, their arrival for the party had been significantly delayed. Despite this, they had managed to reach the party a couple of hours before it fully kicked off. Their presence, though a bit belated, was like a breath of fresh air.

Christy handed over the microphone to Andrei, signaling that it was time for him to share his own tales from the high seas. The atmosphere buzzed with anticipation as Andrei took the stage, ready to recount his adventures and experiences from life aboard the vessel.

For Andrei, the small mic felt as heavy as an anchor in his hand. He looked around at the faces gathered before him, took a deep breath, and began speaking, his thick Bulgarian accent tinged with a mix of pride and deep emotion.

ANDREI – Served as the Third Officer on the *MV Kurasova*

"Thank you very much, Christy, Willy, and Juan, for arranging this get-together. I am very proud to sit here with you all," he began, his voice steady. "But when it comes to sharing a memory—well, that's another matter. I'm still finding my sea legs, so to speak. I haven't been at this long enough to accumulate many tales. Yet, there's one story I hold close, one that shaped my entire life."

Bijoy remembered his first impression of Andrei, who had joined the *MV Kurasova* as the third officer. On that first day, Andrei, a relatively junior officer, didn't stand out in any significant way. However, as time went on, the other crew members had to revise their initial impression of him. Andrei proved himself through his meticulous work ethic and unwavering dedication. He approached his duties with great care, and what truly set him apart was his willingness to ask questions and seek clarification from anyone on-board, regardless of their rank or position.

Andrei stood on the stage, hesitating, the depth of the past visible in his eyes. "Seven years ago in Bulgaria, I was on the brink of achieving my dream. I had completed all my tests and tasks, passed every exam with flying colors. I was ready to put on that first golden stripe on my shoulder and step into the world as a navigation officer. It was my moment—my dream within reach."

Andrei's voice grew somber as he spoke, his eyes clouded with the weight of the memory. "But fate had other plans. My father—my rock, my hero, the one who always wanted to see me in uniform—suffered a terrible accident at the sawmill where he worked. A heavy log fell on him, leaving him paralyzed. In an instant, my world came crashing down."

He paused, taking a deep breath to steady himself. "I had to put my dreams on hold to care for him. I took up any job I could find—working at the same sawmill where he had been injured, cleaning tables in a restaurant, managing a storeroom. Anything that would allow me to be home every evening, to be there for him."

The lawn fell silent as Andrei's voice faltered. "For three long years, I did everything I could, but despite my best efforts, he passed away. The loss was devastating. I learned the hardest lessons about sacrifice and the unpredictable turns life can take."

He paused, visibly struggling with his emotions. "With him gone, reality hit me hard. I had to return to the sea, but the dream I had been chasing seemed out of reach. No one wanted to take me as a trainee officer, let alone an officer. So, I started again, this time as a trainee seaman, working under the bosun, working hard on deck, all the while looking at the navigation bridge and other officers, with tears in my eyes."

Everyone in the audience seemed to hold their breath as Andrei continued, "One blistering hot day, as I was painting the exterior wall of the navigation bridge, drenched in sweat and exhaustion, the captain called out to me. 'Hey, seaman, come here!' His voice cut through the noise of the wind and the sea."

Andrei's eyes flashed with the intensity of that moment. "I ran to him, my heart racing."

'Andrei, are you an officer?' he asked, his tone almost curious.

I hesitated for a moment before replying, 'Sir, I have the qualifications, but I'm currently a trainee seaman.'

His brow furrowed slightly. 'Why are you a trainee seaman if you're qualified to be an officer?' he asked. His voice was steady and devoid of judgment.

I had seen him many times in the distance, but this was the first time that I spoke with him. He had the reputation of being a captain who never practiced any rank discrimination. At sixty, he was still incredibly energetic, a dynamic presence on the ship. He had a genuine passion for teaching and shaping junior officers, always eager to pass on his wisdom and help them grow.

I shared my life story with him, laying bare the dream I had to set aside because of my father's injury. I spoke of how his accident had forced me to pause my aspirations and focus on his care. The weight of those years, the sacrifices made, and the unfulfilled ambitions were all there in my words.

'I saw your certificates in the document file.'"

Andrei's voice trembled as he recalled the captain's response. His eyes glistened with unshed tears as he recounted the moment. "Then Captain Avi Lugasi said something that changed my life forever. He told me, 'Come to the navigation bridge in clean clothes right away. You will train under me for the next two months. If you prove yourself, I'll promote you.'

I was overwhelmed, tears streaming down my face. The bosun, seeing my state, gave me a quick hug and urged me to hurry."

Andrei took a deep breath, his voice barely more than a whisper. "For the next two months, Captain Avi was relentless. He pushed me to my limits—teaching, scolding, and molding me into an officer. It was grueling, but his belief in me never wavered. At the end of those two months, he kept his promise and promoted me to an officer." Andrei finished with a pause.

Anna, sitting in the front row, said, "The captain could have easily overlooked your qualifications, keeping you on deck and carrying on with his day. But he saw beyond that—he recognized a person worthy of a chance, regardless of the circumstances. His choice was a remarkable act of kindness."

When Andrei returned to his table, his girlfriend enveloped him in a tight embrace, her kiss soft and comforting. With gentle hands, she helped him wipe away the tears that had slipped down his cheeks. In that moment, surrounded by the warmth of her support and the appreciation of those around him, Andrei felt a profound sense of positivity and gratitude.

Music continued to play loudly; the night was meant to be celebrated.

Amol was riding high on the energy of the party, his gray jacket and white round-collar t-shirt giving him a charismatic presence. With his lively spirit, he flitted around the chairs, dancing with every shift in the music, and his enthusiasm showed no signs of waning even after midnight.

When Andrei finished his story, Amol's excitement was palpable. He stood up, his face partly shaded by his hand, and called out, "Should I come to the stage?" He then paused for a moment before adding with a grin, "Actually, I'm more comfortable talking here at the table."

Willy chuckled at Amol's playful tone. He approached his table and handed him the microphone. "The stage is all yours, Amol—sorry, I mean, the table is all yours," he corrected himself with a grin.

AMOL – Served as the Second Officer on the *MV Kurasova*

Amol took the mic and addressed the gathered guests. "Well, I've heard all the incredible stories and experiences tonight, and I'm trying to grasp just how fortunate I am to be here. I didn't face much struggle getting into this career. The sea and sky were always my dreams, even as a child."

"My father was a teacher, deeply passionate about observing the stars and constellations. During our evening walks on the beach near the school where he taught, he would regale me with stories—tales of stars, impossible human feats, and daring sea expeditions.

I remember when my father showed me the Hale-Bopp comet in the sky. He told me that the next time humans would witness the same comet, around 2,400 years would have passed. Can you imagine? 2,400 years and none of us will be here to witness it."

He smiled, lost in the memory. "He taught me to identify the pole star and explained that it represents the imaginary axis of the Earth. He would say that if you watch closely, you could see the pole star fixed in one position while all the other stars seem to revolve around it as the Earth rotates. I was a kid at that time, but later, when I joined the ship, I was able to connect everything that he had taught me about stars and the sky. Those moments, those lessons, slowly nurtured my own love for the stars and navigation."

"And now, here I am, carrying forward that passion," he said, with a flourish.

"On my first day on the ship, I had a very special and unforgettable experience. For lunch, the chief cook served a chicken curry that tasted worse than anything I'd ever encountered. Yet, there was a strange pride in his eyes, as if he was showing off his talent for making this Indian dish—for the only Indian on-board. He even claimed to know over a thousand Indian recipes. I thought to myself, 'Well, I'm going to need a lot more time on this ship to try them all.'

The next day, he served 'chicken curry' again. This time, it was even worse! After a week of enduring this same unpalatable dish for both lunch and dinner, I finally had to put my foot down. I told him, 'Never make this dish again. And if you do, at least call it by some other name, not chicken curry.'

From then on, he barely spoke to me until he completed his time on-board."

Amol's humorous story and narration style were getting a few chuckles from the audience.

"But the Captain was too good," Amol continued, "Captain Felix—I still remember him clearly, and the distinct smell of the cigars he used to smoke. He was a vastly experienced Polish captain. Celestial navigation was his specialty, and I was fortunate to fall into the right hands."

Amol's eyes sparkled with amusement as he continued. "He taught me how to use the sextant, how to determine the ship's position using stars and celestial objects, and how to study the sky to predict weather. It was both fascinating and complex. The only challenge was his English. He spoke whatever came to his mind—no grammar, no structure. It took me a while to fully grasp what he was explaining."

Amol, known for his talent for telling funny stories with a straight face, carried on. "We had this compass repeater at the bridge wing—a tall pillar-like device with a compass inside. It was used for taking celestial observations and readings. And, of course, it was always covered with canvas to protect it from bad weather."

He paused, a mischievous glint in his eye. "The captain was very protective of that equipment. Some nights, after his daily quota of vodka, I'd see him talking to the compass repeater and even kissing it gently, as if he thought it was a living creature. He'd be hallucinating, treating it like his dear friend."

The room erupted in laughter as Amol mimicked the captain's endearing eccentricity, his serious expression adding life to the story.

"One fine morning, around nine, I was working with the bosun on deck, de-rusting the vertical ladder. You know the routine—earmuffs on, eyes shielded with glasses, and covered in dust from the rust. I was dirty all over."

He paused for effect. "Suddenly, the captain's voice crackled over the radio. 'Amol, come to the navigation bridge right now!' He sounded furious.

I ran to the bridge, leaving everything on deck. Instead of the elevator, I took the stairs, climbing up ten floors. When I finally reached the bridge wing, I saw the captain and the chief officer standing there, examining the compass repeater. The canvas had been removed, and they were checking inside."

Amol's expression grew serious as he described the encounter. "The captain turned to me and asked, 'Amol, who discovered this?' His voice was stern. I was panting, barely able to catch my breath. The captain was the kind of person who liked to quiz us cadets and always expected at least half an answer. But this time, I was completely at a loss."

He mimicked the captain's demanding tone, "'Cadet, I am asking you, who discovered this one?' His voice was more profound and authoritative this time.

"Thomas Alva Edison, Sir Isaac Newton, even Galileo flashed through my mind, but I had no idea who was behind the invention of the compass. I was racing, trying to come up with an answer."

Amol paused the story for a moment, looking around at the audience. "Does anyone know who discovered the compass?"

The guests exchanged puzzled glances. Rajesh looked over at Bijoy, raising his eyebrows in a silent question. Bijoy shook his head, indicating he didn't know either.

Amol grinned, enjoying the suspense he'd created. "Okay, ladies and gentlemen, don't think too hard about it," he continued with a chuckle. "I discovered the compass!"

Gregory commented, "Oh Amol, you are too high and drunk." It was clear that Gregory had missed the point of the humorous story, but Amol just smiled and continued with his narrative.

"The captain handed me the canvas cover and told me, 'Cover it now.' I took the cover, wrapped it around the compass repeater, and secured it with a small rope."

He imitated the captain's animated gesture. "'Next time you discover this equipment, make sure you cover it back. Otherwise, it will be kaput!'"

Amol paused before continuing. "Oh, God, his special English! What he meant was, 'Who removed the cover?'— 'dis-covered' it, as he put it. Then it finally hit me—I'd forgotten to cover the compass the night before, and it had sustained minor damage due to the rain."

The audience roared with laughter, appreciating Amol's skillful blending of humor and a real-life lesson. His playful recounting of the captain's unique English.

After the cheerful laughter from his previous story, Amol continued with a twinkle in his eye. "I was a bit overenthusiastic on my first ship, always eager to jump into action before I fully understood what was going on."

'That you are, even now,' said Bijoy from the audience.

Amol leaned in slightly, his tone becoming more animated. "One day, I was on the navigation bridge helping the second officer when the captain came in and asked us, 'Have you seen the electrician anywhere?'"

"We both said 'no.'"

"Then the captain started talking to the second officer while I, eager to prove myself, bolted out of the bridge to find the electrician. I searched the engine room, the mess room, and the accommodation – he was nowhere to be found. Finally, I spotted him up on the forward mast, about fifteen meters high, working on the navigation light."

He paused, the audience hanging on his every word. "I stood there, below the mast, and shouted up to him, 'Hey, electrician, the captain's calling you. Emergency!'

Amol mimicked the electrician's irritated response. "'What emergency?' he asked, tied onto a lifeline and burning under the sun, just wanting to finish that minor repair.

Amol continued, 'I don't know. He's waiting for you.'

The electrician climbed down in a hurry, leaving his job half-done, and rushed to the navigation bridge."

He took a dramatic breath. "When we arrived, I presented him to the captain. The captain looked surprised and asked, 'Yes, electrician, tell me.'"

Amol's voice took on a mock-serious tone, "'Did you call me, captain? What is the emergency?'"

Amol's expression shifted to one of embarrassment. "The captain looked at me, still standing there with the pride of having fulfilled his command.

'Where were you working?' the captain asked the electrician.

'On the forward mast,' the electrician replied.

He grinned, finishing the story with a flourish. "'I was looking for some new movies to watch tonight. Nothing urgent,' the captain said. 'And this joker ran to you without listening properly.'"

Amol laughed as he recalled the electrician's reaction. "Hearing this, I just hid behind the second officer while the electrician started letting loose at me in his native language. Thankfully, I didn't understand a word."

The room erupted in laughter, enjoying Amol's impeccable storytelling and vivid re-enactments. The mood had shifted to a jovial one, and no one seemed to notice the time. The night was too enjoyable to end anytime soon.

Rohit's teasing voice cut through the laughter. "Amol, tell us about the story when Bosun took you for a Thai massage in China for the first time."

Amol folded his hands dramatically as if to run away.

Rajesh chimed in, "And what about the time you missed the ship because you were busy partying in Savannah?"

Amol raised his hands in a mock surrender. "Sir, I didn't actually miss the ship. Yes, the ship had already sailed when I got back to the port, but the coastguard kindly drove me out to the ship while it was still in the river."

He chuckled, adding, "So technically, I didn't miss it. Just a little late to the party—a little expensive party."

The crowd roared with laughter, clearly enjoying Amol's witty responses and good-natured storytelling. Despite the lateness of the hour, everyone was eager to hear more.

Finally, Amol said, "Now I am done. Let's hear from someone else."

Christy returned to the stage, his smile lighting up the party's atmosphere, making it even more relaxed and enjoyable. "I can hear some snoring from the corners," he teased, glancing around with a mischievous grin. "I know it's close to two in the morning, but come on, let's have one more story before we call it a night."

He paused for effect before adding, "Now, let's hear a story from the superman himself." His voice was playful yet inviting as he walked over to the table where Rohit, his wife Paro, and Amol were seated. His eyes sparkled with curiosity, eager to draw out the next tale from Rohit's adventures.

"How was your parachute jump yesterday?" he asked Rohit.

"Oh, it was fantastic! Thank you for arranging it for us," Rohit replied, still glowing from the thrill. Christy had orchestrated this adventure, a dream they had put on hold from their last trip to Auckland, when they arrived on the *MV Kurasova* with three survivors.

"Bravo!" Rajesh chimed in, humor in his voice. "Feeling like Tom Cruise?"

"Absolutely! The free fall, the sensation of weightlessness, the wind spinning around—well, not completely free. I was strapped to the trainer, after all," Rohit said, grinning.

Christy leaned in slightly, his tone shifting to something more serious. "So, what superman moments are you sharing with us tonight? I remember that jump you made to save Juan. Wasn't that almost suicidal? What was going through your mind at the time?"

Rohit chuckled, shaking his head. "Honestly, I wasn't thinking at all. Maybe that's what gave me the courage— a brain on autopilot."

"Come on, come on," Christy urged, stepping back and gesturing for Rohit to join him on the stage.

The crowd erupted into applause, chanting "Rohit… Rohit…" as the six-foot-tall, broad-shouldered man made his way to the stage.

"Tell us, Rohit," Christy said, his voice softening as the atmosphere hushed in anticipation. "One incident from your sea life that stands out. Not the rescue mission, though."

Rohit paused; the room was silent as he gathered his thoughts. Then, with a deep breath, he began.

ROHIT – Served as the Third Engineer on the *MV Kurasova*

"For many of us, the first day on-board is a memory etched in time," he started, his voice wavering with emotion.

"Amol and I were batchmates at nautical school, captivated by the Merchant Navy's allure and the call of the sea. My selection by a reputable company filled me with pride, a feeling that only intensified as I clutched my first plane ticket, waving goodbye to my parents with a mix of excitement and trepidation.

I never imagined that the pangs of separation would cut so deep. As the flight descended towards

Rotterdam, my joining port, a gnawing ache settled in. I began to miss home in a way I hadn't anticipated.

Upon arrival, the agent whisked me away to the ship. Loneliness gnawed at me with every passing moment. The long flight, the car journey with a stranger, and the endless port formalities made it feel like I was heading to a place of confinement rather than adventure. Then, I saw it—my first ship.

Majestic and imposing, it stood like a giant metal fortress, my home for the next nine months. As the first from my batch to join, I was completely unaware of what life on-board truly entailed. With luggage in tow, I ascended the steep gangway, each step heavier than the last. And then, I was aboard.

A towering figure clad in a boilersuit, with a black bandanna tied around his head, stood before me, his imposing presence softened by a broad grin.

'Welcome on board, Cadet,' he greeted warmly.

I stammered out a reply, the overwhelming scent of metal and oil filling my nostrils, the deafening hum of the engine reverberating in my chest. He guided me to the ship's office, where the oppressive atmosphere intensified. The narrow alleyways, the incessant noise—it felt as if I was being swallowed by a tunnel."

The audience listened to Rohit with rapt attention.

"Inside the office, I anxiously scanned the crew list, hoping to find a familiar name, perhaps another Indian, but the unknown names on the list only deepened my sense of isolation. I was alone, truly alone.

The Chief Engineer arrived, a burly man with long hair at the back, his bulky face framed by a Russian-style boilersuit.

'How was your trip?' he asked gruffly.

'It was okay, Sir,' I managed.

'Have you eaten?'

'No, Sir.'

'Come with me.'

He led me to the mess room, where a few crew members were already seated for dinner. He introduced me, but my mind was elsewhere, lost in the labyrinth of my own thoughts.

My first meal on-board was a blur. I could not even recall what I ate, nor did I eat much. My thoughts drifted back to home, to everything I had left behind.

'Get some rest. We're departing the port soon, so see you tomorrow morning in the Engine Control Room,' the Chief Engineer said before leaving me in the mess room.

Then a Croatian steward led me to my cabin on the fourth deck. It was a compact space – a single bunk, a small table and chair, and a tiny shelf for my belongings.

As the steward closed the door behind him, a wave of suffocation hit me. Anxiety clawed at me, a gnawing doubt about the path I had chosen. Why had I opted for a career that would isolate me from family, surround me with strangers, and confine me to a steel ship for months? The thought of not setting foot on solid ground for so long weighed heavily on my mind.

I walked to the small window and opened it. Outside, the bustle of the port continued unabated. Containers swung through the air, suspended by cranes as they were loaded onto the ship.

I lay down on the bed, the day's events swirling in my head. Despite the turmoil inside, exhaustion eventually overtook me, and sleep claimed me without warning.

I woke with a sudden start. Rushing to the window, I saw the lights of the port fading into the distance. I was wondering what I should do now.

I decided to take a hot shower, the best place to cry and let my mind wander.

Ten minutes in the shower and suddenly, *Tring... tring....* My room phone started ringing, jolting me out of the bathroom. My foot hit a corner hard.

"Hello," I said, through my pain.

'Who are you?' an angry voice demanded.

'Sir, Engine Cadet Rohit,' I stammered.

'Whoever you are, close your bloody windows. You're disturbing the navigation!' The rude voice slammed down the phone.

I closed the window quickly, realizing that the light from the accommodation spaces can disturb the night navigation. Another layer added to my misery. An embarrassment on the first day. I finished my shower and returned to bed, heavy-hearted. Homesickness peaked, and I could not hold back the tears, perhaps louder than I intended.

Suddenly, a loud bang came from my bedside wall.

'Stop it, you idiot. I want to sleep!' an angry voice from the next room shouted.

"You know how thin the walls are on ships," Rohit said to the crowd, pulling their minds back from the ship.

"Yeah, you sneeze or fart, and your neighbor hears it," Amol commented, trying to lighten the mood. But everyone was looking at Rohit seriously, especially Paro, who had never seen this side of him.

Rohit continued, "Momentarily, I fell silent. But I couldn't hold it for long. I was weeping again.

After a while, a faint tap came on the wall—the same wall, but this time it wasn't a bang. It was gentle, almost like a hesitant knock.

I didn't respond.

'First time on-board, eh?' a voice with a thick accent came from the next room.

'Yes, first day on a ship,' I replied.

'Welcome aboard, Seaman,' the voice was soft, as if the anger had vanished.

I didn't say anything.

'Missing home?'

'Yes, very much.'

'Do you want to go home?'

I didn't respond.

'Oh boy, every seaman goes through this emotion at some point. The first day on a ship will be like this. You'll laugh at this after a few months. By the time you go home, you'll be a man. A man capable of anything. A seaman.'

After a pause, he continued, 'We're a group of twenty-five men on-board. There are no nationalities here. We're all here to serve the good lady, our ship. Do you understand?'

'Yes, Sir,' I said.

'Don't call me sir. Be strong. Let the days pass, and you'll become strong.'

"Okay, I'll be strong.'

'That's a good boy. Tell me, do you have a girlfriend?'
he asked.

"No,' I said.

'What?' he said in surprise. 'How many broken bones
do you have?'

'None,' I said proudly.

'How old are you?'

'I'm 23.'

'Oh man, what a waste. What have you been doing
with your life? No girlfriends, no broken bones. A life
without action,' he teased.

The conversation boosted my spirits.

'Life as a seaman is a journey of endless horizons and
adventures. Each day brings the beauty of sunrises
over vast oceans and nights under a canopy of stars.
You travel around the world, meet many people, and
make a lot of money,' he continued.

For the first time in twenty-four hours, I felt proud of
choosing the life of a seaman.

Finally, after about an hour of conversation, I asked, 'What's your name?'

'I'm Danijel. You can call me Danny,' he paused and said, 'Okay, good night. Sleep tight.'

'Okay, good night. What's your rank?' I asked.

'I am the bosun.'

'Where are you from?'

'I told you earlier, there are no nationalities here, just seamen.' He paused and said, 'Now you get some sleep, we will talk tomorrow.'

The next morning, I got up, showered, and rushed to the mess room. I considered knocking on Danny's door but realized I didn't know his duty hours. Maybe he was sleeping.

I greeted everyone and headed to the Engine Control Room with newfound pride. I felt like a new man after that first night on-board.

'Good morning, Sir,' I greeted the chief engineer as I entered the Engine Control Room.

'Good morning, Cadet. How are you?' he asked.

'Good, Sir.'

'He introduced me to the other crew members and outlined safety precautions.

'Remember, your life is your responsibility. Stamp that into your mind,' he told me.

I took his words to heart, bolstered by my conversation with Danny.

Oh, I forgot to ask about him.

"Sir, who is staying in the room next to mine?"

'The next room? I think it's empty,' the chief engineer paused, then turned to the second engineer for confirmation. 'Isn't that room empty?'

'Right now, the room is just a storage space for old logbooks and stationery,' the second engineer replied in a flat tone. 'No one's used it since that unfortunate accident with the bosun.'

'Empty? Accident?' I exclaimed.

'Ha ha, are you afraid?' the chief engineer laughed, and the others joined in.

'We had a bosun many years back on this ship, Danijel, or Danny. He was rough but exceptionally good for his rank,' the chief engineer said, his tone somber. 'Unfortunately, he died in a mooring accident during some bloody bad weather in Rotterdam. The mooring rope snapped and hit him hard, breaking almost every bone in his body. A truly terrible way to die. No one used that room after the incident.'"

Rohit paused his story, letting the silence stretch for a couple of minutes. He scanned the audience, noticing that many were staring with their mouths agape. Lewis was in shock. Everyone exchanged uneasy glances, struggling to believe if what they had just heard was the truth or simply a haunting myth.

When the silence extended, Christy stepped in; his voice, though firm, had an undertone of warmth and appreciation as he addressed the gathering. "Alright, gentlemen. Thank you so much for your wonderful stories, but it is three in the morning now. The night is no longer young. Let us wind up here. I know there are many questions in your minds. We'll catch Rohit tomorrow for answers."

TIME TO SAY 'AU REVOIR'

As the night wound down, a gentle hush fell over the garden, the air thick with the remnants of laughter. Guests rose from their seats, exchanging warm hugs and heartfelt farewells, their smiles illuminated by the soft glow of twinkling fairy lights. Sofia and Robert, ever the gracious hosts, guided their departing friends to the waiting cars, their spirits buoyed by the evening's camaraderie.

The echoes of joyous chatter began to fade, replaced by the soft rustle of leaves swaying in the night breeze. The heroes, the valiant crew of the *MV Kurasova*, embarked on their journey home, hearts still alight with the stories shared and the bonds forged.

As the last car pulled away, Juan, Christy and Willy lingered, reluctant to break the spell of the evening. They stood together, gazing out over the now quiet garden, their thoughts swirling like the leaves around them. The flickering lights, though still radiant, felt like stars beginning to dim at dawn, signaling the end of an extraordinary chapter.

Their eyes drifted toward a prominent display of photographs, each frame a window into their past adventures on the Pacific Ocean. The images fluttered slightly in the cool breeze. Then, one photo caught their collective breath – a striking image of the entire crew, captured in a moment of triumph on the jetty. The *MV Kurasova* loomed behind them, majestic and powerful, like a proud mother watching over her children.

Epilogue II

Once a Sailor, Always a Sailor

GALLE FORT
SRILANKA

"Dad, shall we go? It's getting late. You promised me a jungle safari today," Amiya's eager voice cut through Bijoy's thoughts like a knife through mist. She stood before him, her new gray jungle suit a perfect fit, and her eyes wide with anticipation.

Bijoy blinked, his mind snapping back to the present. "What time is it?" he muttered, as though the day had suddenly slipped past him.

They were here for a five-day vacation to immerse themselves in the beauty of Sri Lanka, a much-awaited break after his exhausting contract on-board the ship. This time together felt precious, especially with Amiya starting school in a month, leaving fewer opportunities for such adventures.

Priya, sensing the familiar distant look in his eyes, stepped closer and placed a reassuring hand on his arm. "Don't worry, sweetheart," she said gently, her voice imbued with warmth and understanding. "We have all the time in the world."

Yet, beneath her soothing words, Priya knew that Bijoy's thoughts were far from the present moment, drifting back to the sea that had shaped so much of his life. She could almost see the vivid tapestry of his seafaring experiences unfolding in his mind—stories she had come to know intimately, often recounted as she rested her head on his chest, listening to the steady rhythm of his heartbeat.

She imagined him standing proudly in New Zealand, receiving the valiant award for rescuing three men from the tumultuous ocean—a moment of recognition that symbolized his courage. She could feel the awe that had filled him during the epic circumnavigation, an inspiring journey that took him 360 degrees around the globe in seventy days.

Her heart tightened as she recalled the time when he spoke of outrunning Somali pirates, his voice steady but laced with the fear he rarely showed. And then there were the tears he had shed in silence; tears she had wiped away as he mourned not being able to attend his beloved mother's funeral since he was on-board a ship—an absence that had cut deeper than any storm he had weathered at sea.

Priya's thoughts lingered on the months he had been stranded on-board, when the world had locked down due to the contagious virus that had captured everyone in its grip. Then there were the lighter memories—images of equator-crossing ceremonies where he had been painted in colorful, humorous designs, laughter filling the air as he embraced the playful traditions of the sea.

She was proud of the man he was—the captain who had faced down the elements, the husband who had remained faithful to both the sea and to her, the father who was trying, with all his might, to be present.

"Give me fifteen minutes," Bijoy finally said.

He turned sharply, made his way to the bedroom, his steps as precise and determined as if he were still pacing the deck of a ship. Even on solid ground, the ocean's rhythm never left him.

Priya watched him disappear behind the door. She knew that no matter how far inland they ventured, a part of Bijoy would always remain adrift, forever tied to the vast, untamed waters. But she also knew that, for now, they had him here—fully, undeniably present.

THE END